AF419918

# DHARMA BOARDS
## Revolution – Part II

JUSTIN DALRYMPLE-KELLY

Dharmaboards@gmail.com

Facebook @ Dharma Boards Productions
Dharma Boards Manifesto Pt. 1 & 2 Audio Books can be accessed at: https;//m.youtube.com@Dharma Boards Productions

# <u>Act VI</u>

# Chapter 32

The disembodied head of Marcus took two dampened thuds across the stone and rolled oblong into the corner. It took its place beside the head of Klatos, pale, that lay at bloods end, red trail smudge.

"I'm not gonna waste my time," said Synthia "with any more chatter."

Playfully she rolled the head beneath her toes with such finesse. She turned away, took a few steps to the wall and placed a cold iron board, sharp, against the wall. From the guillotine the blood still dripped onto the floor.

Synthia sat, expelled a long cold sigh from within her bones. She folded her arms upon the table. She looked within, alone, within a chamber of the earth. Her stare is disembodied, she isn't there. She didn't need to plug into a glowing ball above her head for this rumination. These are thoughts below the words, beneath any images, the brooding forces of her dreamless sleep. The cogs of the machine within her evil mind are turning.

She stood, running a slow hand against the smooth stone wall. Perhaps it's smooth while other stones are not because she's been through this before. She is wearing this disguise, she calls it Synthia. She's just another evil spirit from the crack of the dawn of time.

"I don't need anyone!" Synthia yelled out loud. "I never have. And that's the last time I do anyone a favor. Or is my deep subconscious mind, my door to evil sources itself providing— yes— I, Synthia— I am not in charge of this. For what am I, but minutes of a walking conscious demon? No. I am but an instrument of that which calls itself evil. I am aligned with its intentions and it has blessed me with a solution to my problem, of a wretched business partner and his assistant, not to mention it. Yes, she has delivered me from co-ruler ship, so that I can—," she stopped.

"Yes," she said, as she turned in the darkness. "Yes. It's all coming to me now. I knew it would— praise evil. No…, praise *darkness*."

She knelt. She bowed. She was exited. She traversed across a series of illuminated skywalks. Some protruded in the night air under stars among the forest, and some among the annals of the bedrock of the mountain. Synthia mentally transverse aloof, and well at ease in this amount of power she had entered into in her psyche. She all but floated into a metal chamber. Here upon this room are walls of forfeiting metal, blue-grey, silver in their hue, and almost luminescent in the darkness. It is a dome of simple form. But within these walls there is an eerie hum. A mixture of a supersonic pitch combined with undulating lower registers unheard by humans. There were several small experimental areas and things marked off by curtains.

Synthia sat down at a computer, entering a sequence on the screen, which triggered some equipment in the space to operate.

"Yes," Synthia said. "Yes, oh, yes it comes together now."

The chamber has a single chamber that descends upon the center of the space. One solid, black, cylindrical tube, created from the same jet black windows of the dark façade outside.

Now Synthia completes the sequence and initiates the operation with a single stroke of the final enter key and waits.

The jet black cylinder releases pressure, gas and lights flicker on the ceiling as heir Synthia looks up. Another high expulsion sound comes from the glass and Synthia snaps her attention back onto the vestibule with a jerk of her neck and her head. Her eyes are bulging with lack of oxygen, her adrenaline and senses are heightened, one for recognition of impression of this moment, and one for any microscopic detail she can eat up with her evil soul.

The cylinder, silently, slowly, actuates.

Synthia quivers. A man dressed in black, synthetic, extraterrestrial, and ancient leather, steps out of the jet black cylinder. His façade is hidden beneath a leather mask with jet black portholes for his eyes. It is clear he is no man, no woman, and no machine. He is something else. The machine is close enough. But more like the machine of cosmological implications, embodied in materials of optimized performance. He is perfect in every way. He is a man of darkness. There is no heart beneath his chest. There is no mind within his head. He is Synthia's creation. And she will have her way with him.

He stepped forward into the light from the obscurity of the tube. He took two steps down the tinkering metal stand that the cylinder is seated on, and stared ahead as straight as night. There was emptiness beyond all emptiness within his gaze, for cold cannot describe it.

Synthia ran her hand across his chest as she circumnavigated his body.

"Yes," she said. "Oh yes. I think you'll do."

The frozen gaze of him is undetected by anything that might have sensors, for a creature, or a being. Undetected like the death of some museum prop, but he moved with some volition and it wasn't... natural.

"Come," said Synthia, in a whisper. "We have work to do."

# Chapter 33

"The United Riders have been summoned," Zeddefungo said. "We will see you soon."

Dharma made her way down the Rainer staircase. Maya was waiting in the kitchen.

"How are you feeling?" Maya asked.

"Better," Dharma said. "Much better." Dharma couldn't help looking out the picture window in the living room. Maya arrived at her side. Dharma looked at her and put an arm around her in comfort.

"Everything is in ruins," Maya said.

"It will be okay." Dharma consoled her.

"How can you say that?" Maya asked.

"I have the privilege and the curse of seeing many things like this, though, not this bad, I admit," Dharma said. "But we must stay positive. It will be a long road, and an uphill hill one, to rebuilding. But in the end it will be better than it ever was before."

Maya continued looking out the window at the winter disarray, with smokestacks in the distance like a forest.

"Zeddefungo said that they will meet us along the way," said David Rainer upon entering the room.

"Zeddefungo?" asked Adam, interested, and following in his father's footsteps. "Where're we going?"

"We need to meet with the United Riders," answered David. "A crisis this big needs to be addressed. We can manage as we always do, but need to get together to see what exactly has happened here."

Maya and Dharma shared a responsible look.

"Cool," said Adam. "Where's it at?"

"Adam," said Maya. "Why are you so flippant? Can't you see the world as we all know it just ended?" Maya held her arm up towards the window.

"Flippant?" Adam asked. "I didn't ask to have abilities to flip so well, but what's that got to do with the apocalypse?"

Maya stared at him somewhat dumbfounded. David Rainer wrestled with the puppy on the carpet 'til it peed on his shirt. David responded with disgust. Maya looked to Dharma who appropriately acknowledged the disbelief of Maya, but just closed her own eyes and walked over to Maya.

"Some people process things differently," Dharma said.

"You mean not at all?" asked Maya.

"It would appear that way," Dharma answered. "Never you mind. We all have our roles."

David smelled his wet shirt.

"Now, pack your things everyone," announced Dharma. "We're going on a family trip."

"Oh dear," David said.

"We don't have any things," said Adam.

"Good, well then let's get a move on," Dharma said. "No time to waste."

From the rubble of the city of Detroit, the riders passed through an Old Oak Tree in the Arboretum of the University of Michigan. This transport point hurried them along to some Old Oak Tree in Roanoke, a Colony in West Virginia— North Carolina rather, on an island. On the tree were the markings of long lost settlers' remains.

"Sister!" Zeddefungo said cheerfully as he rushed up her to hug her.

Tjikko greeted the newest Chris— or David rather with a fist bump. "Chris," Tjikko nodded.

"Tjikko,—uh it's David," said David.

"What's David, Chris?" Tjikko asked.

"My name," said David.

"Oh, well— David," Tjikko nodded again. "Thanks for taking care of my sister. Real hero stuff— I swear I know you— okay, let's go, we are late!"

The group of riders set out in a southeastern direction on the Atlantic sea. The day was grey and gloomy and they passed as distant vessels, jet skis, or anything. They continued in this way, heading for what seemed like quite a while, before they took a slight veer left at Dharma's lead.

"You guys," said Zeddefungo, "We have to ride like the sea of life. Mimic something's movements like a dolphin" he said, floundering. "Or else they'll see the anomaly on the scanners. Somebody. Right?"

"Sure thing, Zefu," Tjikko said. "You do your little dolphin swim."

Tjikko laughed with fondness at his brother.

"Where are we *going*?" Adam asked, as he stared into the blue-grey blur of the vanishing horizon.

"The council meets inside a village called— Atlantis," Ubuntu answered.

"Greece?" Maya asked.

"Hawaii." Ubuntu answered, ineffably.

"Hawaii?" Maya asked.

"Hawaii?" Adam asked. "Then why are we off the east coast of Florida?"

"Sometimes you have to go east, to go west..." said Zeddefungo, forebodingly. Then he wriggled off into a dolphin maneuver.

Suddenly, in the distance, a figure took its shape. It was a massive darkened pit within a geometrically concise sharp lined shape— of a colossal triangle. The water falls equally over each of its three edges ran deep into the endless pit. It rushed like the great Niagara Falls times three.

"The Bermuda Triangle," announced Zeddefungo. "The only way to get to Old Atlantis."

"Wow," said Maya in a whisper, staring almost reverently at the triangle.

"I just don't get how no one is seeing this," said Adam, after staring for a disbelieving minute. "Planes, boats, and Google Maps."

"Ah, Adam," Ubuntu answered. "No one is seeking it in the *right way*. You must approach it with a true heart, and with true intentions. Humans seek it for their exploitation, to put it in museums or at tourist traps. But Atlantis hides itself. There are people who don't seek truth, they seek a curse. They will never find it," Ubuntu said, as she floated above the roaring gorge. "The triangle is shy. It hides itself within the folds and creases of the fabric of reality. The three fold gate protects the lost city from unwarranted discoveries.

Maya stared into the ominous chasm, transfixed.

"What are the folds and creases of the fabric made of?" Maya asked.

"Like the prisms of the branches of the leafless trees in winter, or the intersecting of angels on the stalks and cane, though the window figures that you look through need not be on any true straight line," Ubuntu said. "The mind plays tricks on everyone. We agree on lines in space from one perspective, made of points of prism objects 'tween the branches. That's where it goes up for interpretation." Ubuntu finished.

"We just have a different... view," added Dharma.

Everybody looked transfixed. David Rainer blinked his eyes repeatedly and looked around. Tjikko laughed at this.

"Now follow me!" Dharma called, as she entered into the huge abyss.

The scale was like a massive soccer field of darkness. The riders looked like little ants, viewed from the side, as they descended into the unknown. The water gushed all around them. Even Adam had a look of trepidation on his face. The riders shot the gap of blackness in slow motion.

Suddenly a shift in the surroundings came. The light is purple green and blue about the tunnel vortex, they now ride through, fall through, suck through like a fluid like the roots and fungus of the trees delivering them, this aquatic— not a submarine, but transportation on a spirituous-molecule criteria. A parallel dimension. The riders are there and not there, as much as they are eternal and infinite. It's a slide. It's a skippering slithery snake but it's electric, but more primal than electric, it is water. It is liquid. Specifically it is—

"Wooooohoohoo," said Zeddefungo, as they shoot out from under up the other side.

The world is upside down and inside out and they're under the water in the sky, whereas before they were above the sky over the water. The sky is inside out, it's purple. The sun is red orange glowing in the purple aqueous fluttering like ripples on a pond.

The riders slowly finish with the tubular water way surrounding them. Then they walk out in this other stuff, some water they can breathe in, and it's not as restricting in its drag. It's like thick water— rather air but thinner water.

Maya waves her arms a little looking down at them as she is walking.

Adam waves his hands before his face and smiles like a little child.

"Whoa," Adam echoes and articulates. The sound of his voice warbles and is slower in its echo and faster in its destination. Like a quicker bone delivery but with reverb, yes with reverb.

Maya and Adam followed behind David who is equally perplexed. Tjikko, Zefu and Ubuntu walk in front of him, not *as* amazed but beaming and glowing, and happy to be back, like that. Ubuntu smiles warmly and knowingly and confident as she strides on aqueous agenda. Dharma leads the pack, a lone rider in the night. Yeah, she's all about this life.

"Atlantis," Dharma said, as the water hill created a view of glowing purple blue habitation. Gold orange light glowed, extending.

Maya and Adam hugged each other.

At this point David Rainer is having a religious experience.

"It is real," David cried.

"It is real," Dharma whispered, coming to his side. "Stick with me, and you'll see many things you never could imagine, do exist."

The group descended on the liquid hill, which leads to a trail that leads meanderingly, to city gates.

# Chapter 34

The fiery gates to Atlantis opened with a pinch of electricity. The riders drifted into the city and down the streets of gold. On both sides of one main road were dwellings raised above it were a blue and purple pearl hue, and the lower streets were blue and gold and purple. And its inhabitants floated about their lives. Here it is very important to distinguish this from other modes of life, like the surface creatures of the popular world. Now it is dark. The people are in harmony. Harmony is understood. It is not an overt display of kindliness to catch up on your karma score. It is eternally understood. It is a different dimension of communication all together. It is not survival. It is true and everlasting life. It is perfect like the comely feet of the Greek gods.

Maya walks the golden street above the lower comely dwellings, the grandeur of the city of Atlantis lay above her. It is a Hispanic spirit world of an underwater New York. It is everything. At the top of this broad heap of buildings with its dotted lights of stars extending into emptiness in both directions, fading to the sea, sat a palace. Maya spies it as a speckle in her eye as it glimmers shinning in the orange and purple sun.

Dharma notices her gaze.

"The palace of the King," Dharma said, to Maya nicely.

A chariot of creatures swooped down to a landing on the golden road where the riders are walking along. The beasts of water are a sort of swimming dragon. Their luminescent scales shimmer in the sun.

"Is this for us?" Adam imagined, while externally saying it aloud.

The front one of the creatures stared ahead with duty. The second one even indicates that they should enter upon the holy vessel. The carrier is a translucent pearl material. Adam boarded the boat and made a face straight through the sidewalk as he looked at Maya.

Maya boards the vessel and the rest of them follow. Everyone puts on their Royal airs. With a dash and a swerve, the animals guide the sleigh toward the palace of the king.

As soon as the palace walls are entered, the king descends upon his board to meet the riders. His board is of the very same material as is the sled.

"Welcome, welcome, my sweet Boards Men," said the King to his guests.

The King is sort of like a Tjikko but a strong one. He has gills like all Atlanteans. Unlike all of the Atlanteans, he has fierce purple eyes, and other villagers have blue or green or even purple eyes, as he does in rare cases.

"Tjikko! *My* man!" The King says with his booming reverb of an aqueous voice. It enters the heads of the riders and Tjikko's immediately.

"King Swahili!" Tjikko greeted him, with a booming hug. "It has been far too long. It feels good to be back here though, let me tell you."

"Ah, my brother of the board, it is good to have you back, all of you," the King said, as he turned to the group. "It was terrible to hear of the trashiest things that happened on the surface. We have everything down here prepared for the conference, and we hope to calm this great storm."

Ubuntu bowed to King Swahili. King Swahili bowed. Maya, Dharma, Adam, and Zeddefungo, followed with a bow, and David too.

"Welcome, please, the committee awaits your arrival," said the King.

The King implied *and* gestured them to follow him deeper into the palace where a procession of the eternals was already underway. From the high door in the court above the staircase descending like a massive whale fin, the riders viewed this procession and looked on, some with looks of humbleness and appreciation for life, some with awe and reverie, some completely and utterly amazed, some just joyous to be here, thankful, and grateful.

The procession of the eternals is something to see. The representatives of the Seven Continents and the Ten Rider Zones and the Seventeen Realms, each and every entity has a flag and a Flag Rider. Just then the two Angel Riders arrived with their flaming swords that guard the Gates of Eden. The rest of them are regular enough in their Entity Ships regarding South America— Mercedes Belho, Asia Minor— Jao Zūn, Tjikko's evil Russian cousin, Grigory, and his beautiful and sweet sister, Marie, who stands for all that's good and holy. There are twenty four committee members who all together form the core team of the committee.

When the procession and the entrance are ended everybody took their seats upon the oval table, for there are no chairs. Everybody sat with crossed legs on the table under water in the blue translucent gem jade walls of the palace conference hall. The floor appeared to be checkerboard squares of alternating color squares of creamy orange and creamy white, all opaque and pale and rich in the texture of its stone, and polished. There stood six idols on each checkerboard square pattern on the side that each representing a transcendent legendary warrior of old. Though legendary, and of old, are not correct as they, transcendent, do not exist in this dimension, they exist only in the land of pure ideas where Plato lives. For, any legend, and anyone of old, is alive, and is here now, sitting on this table. For this committee, these United Riders, are truly infinite and indestructible, not to mention undefeated.

Slowly, each rider, seated in the circle around the oval table, started to mark the green jade table with the sounding of their boards. For a split second it is a pitter patter but in an instant it is in rhythmic accordance with the law. The spots where their boards mark the table are a smooth but wavy almost rippled sound from the eons of this cadence. Then it putters to a close.

All is quiet in the hall. Dharma rises to the center of the group. Maya and Adam feel their breath go from their bodies as she goes away.

"We are gathered here today," said Dharma in the purity of silence, like it's all one mind and she is just the tongue of this grand organism. "To collaborate, in the global discord, that has been caused upon this earth. This is something we have seen before but never in this scale, and to be honest in this raw capacity. There was nothing orchestrated, nothing congruent about this. It was pure unbridled chaos. The mystery is, and this is what we are here to overcome, is where this power came from; and to keep this thing from ever happening again."

"Amen!" The group yelled in unison.

"Here, here," said Dharma. "Now, it is the work of what we have come to call the hand of Darkness. The question is how it struck so fast, so hard and went unnoticed."

"Who is this behind it all?" The Saint of Egypt called out. "I have seen her in my dreams. She disturbs us with the power of her vibrant eyes of green like lightning crystals, and her hair of unearthly burning flames."

"Who is she?" Dharma asked them.

"Who is she?" Everyone called out.

Dharma looked around at all the commotion.

Suddenly somebody spoke with full conviction. "Her name is Synthia," said Maya, standing up in her place.

Whispers traveled throughout the conference, all the Angel Riders, and the representatives, and all the Saints of the Board were whispering in joy and expectation of the daughter of the greatest rider, Dharma.

"Is this Maya?" They asked in a whisper. "Is this the Maya we have heard of?"

"Her name is Synthia, though I don't know who she is," Maya offered full of courage. "I can attest to the truth of the power of those bright green eyes. I have seen them with my own. She is in accordance with the Dark Boards, for two members of the sect that we all defeated, not too long ago, were with her."

"Somehow she snaked her way into the forefront, and the limelight, of the world of men," added Dharma. "That's what worries me. Instead of only just destroying man, she's using man himself as slaves, and the integral instrument of its own destruction, but furthermore it's worse. It won't end at the destruction of the race, or the planet. If she is left to her own devices, she will turn this beast of demon men alchemy outwards, toward the stars, consuming all and everything in its path."

The constituents fell silent at this motion and this sentiment.

"This is our task," continued Dharma. "Brothers and sisters of the board, she is still out there. In the rubble of the earth, she remains. We must defeat her with this blow. We cannot miss. We will need to call upon the entirety of our forces. There is a great disturbance in this silence. We must strike."

# Chapter 35

"You may stay here for some time," King Swahili said beneath the stars in the courtyard of the palace. "The people will rebuild their infrastructure after, surely, some committees of their own. It is not our place to increase the pace of the restoration of their world. Surely if it was, we would tell them— not to do it. Make a tent. Stay under a water fall. For the longest lasting structure and foundation is the absence of one. Right? It is that simple."

"Thank you," Dharma answered. "Your offer is much appreciated."

She looked upon the stars above for a moment; they were fiery white within the water sky.

"We could truly use the soothing nature of these waters for our rehabilitation, after all that's happened on the surface," said Dharma.

"Please, please, have anything you need," King Swahili said, and bowed to Dharma. "My servants, my waters, my home is at your service."

Queen Ashanti of Atlantis entered in her flowing silk gown of the sapphire blue color of the sea. Turquoise and purple accents followed her wave paths in slow motion. Her hair was like a magnificent plume of cumulonimbus jet black storm clouds.

"Dharma," the Queen Ashanti said, as she hugged and kissed her long lost fellow royal heiress. "It is so good to see you. Please have anything you need."

"Ashanti" Dharma said, with a warm reception and embrace.

"But what does this mean, my vague sweet King?" Ashanti asked. "Come, tomorrow and I will set you up with healing chambers, meditation, and the real stuff— we must have a Palace Rider take you on a grand adventure of the forest hills and catacombs. What is better for the soul than wonder and astonishment? We will catch your wounded spirit with our nets and let them bloom into a new direction. Yes, we will recalibrate you like the good old days."

"That sounds amazing, my old friend," said Dharma, glowing with hope, and the fellowship she received. Dharma welcomed feelings of friendship in the face of so much dread. "I will take what I can get," said Dharma, bidding them goodnight.

The riders took their marble, pillared huts that lined the arc about the courtyard. The huts were seated slightly higher on a ledge, to have a little view of gardens of the courtyard, while another view of stars above, and city lights below the palace hill, awaited.

They took their huts and took their walks. Zeddefungo reconvened with Mercedes Belho. The way she giggled, and the way he smiled unlike the usual unruly Zeddefungo, revealed a coy and bashful side of him. This reconvening looked like rekindling was possible.

Now Tjikko walked with King Swahili, and the two appeared thick as thieves. The members of the United Riders lined the courtyard and sprinkled the palace grounds, in evening strolls, and little circular gatherings on the lawn.

The stars shined down among a blue moon of the sea world, different than the moon of man. Statues lined the moon reflecting in the linear infinity pool, with canals that led to each establishment and marble hut within the palace. The linear infinity pool dropped off staying like a slice of living ice inside the waterfall that never hit the ground two thousand feet below the palace in the City Center.

Adam and Maya walked alone.

"I think I'm gonna like this place," said Adam.

"Magical..." said Maya, like a transport passing by as she devoured the environment with her perception.

"I could stay here for a *while*," Adam said, as he ran his hand along a statue.

"That's what you're always saying about these amazing places we end up in," she said, as she laughed.

"We'll it's true that there are twenty lifetimes," Adam continued, "Then I could stay in them all for the length of time I deserve to give them."

Maya smiled. "If that is true, then apparently we could fill a million life times with always fighting bad guys," she said.

"Yeah, well," said Adam. "It's better than...a boring unfulfilling life."

"You know what Adam?" Maya said. "You're actually right." She hugged Adam with playfulness. "But you know, I know it, and you know that I envy your enthusiasm, but..."

"But nothing Maya, you know you got the fierceness of a lion, and I'm with you," said Adam. "I don't know what we'd do if you weren't always so cold blooded."

Adam hugged Maya back with admiration.

"You're right again, my brother," Maya said. "Let's just keep playing both of our roles like mom is always saying. Somehow that intuition is the only way."

Then Queen Ashanti joined them with respect, and told them of the wonders of the history and the mystery of Atlantis.

Ubuntu and Jao Zūn from Asia, have always been good friends. They walked along and traded insights, laughs and wisdom. But the monkey in the middle of the two great lands of Africa and Asia is usually Dharma. But she was busy on a moonlight stroll with David. David was on cloud nine and respectfully happy to be part of such a special meeting of the minds in this miraculous environment.

"I never dreamed I'd see things like this," said David.

"It's great to be back, and to see it through the freshest eyes of you, Maya and Adam," Dharma said. "I couldn't ask for more. I have seen it, but... the effect... what it does to your perspective, your soul, your understanding... it's like you, David, are truly in a new dimension of possibilities."

"I couldn't agree more," said David. He starred not out at the city as Dharma now was, but directly into Dharma's eyes.

She turned to realize this and met his eyes with hers. The spark is real, the butterflies appeared and David saw an opportunity to move to her. He brought his face close with the smoothness of the underwater world, but just as he was about to kiss her there was an angel with a flaming sword beside his head. He paused and the moment disintegrated into thin air.

A second angel came up by the side of Maya with a flaming sword and a board beneath her feet.

"We are the representatives of the Heavenly Hosts and the Thirty Six Realms of the Angel Riders" said the second angel.

"Uriel, Azrael, it is good to finally see you again," said Dharma. "For you I think it's been the longest time."

"Likewise, and the mother sends her blessings to your family," the angel on the left announced. "Please, take this Golden Rose of strength for your abilities."

Uriel produced a Golden Rose of light from within his garments and transitioned it to Dharma who received it with all her grace. Her hair took up a glow of radiant blonde but then it faded out with splendor and a haze.

"Do we know you?" Azrael asked David. "You look very familiar."

"I don't think so," answered David. "Everybody's saying that. Like, literally everybody."

"Do we know you, David Rainer?" Uriel asked. "Yes I think we do."

Now David and Dharma stopped fast in their gaze.

"How do you know his name?" Dharma asked.

"Yes, we know his name and everything about him," said Azrael. "Yes."

David looked extremely startled and confused.

"Please, tell me," David said.

"It is not for us to tell," said one of the angels.

"Perhaps a visit to the wicked mother is in order," said the other angel.

"*Wicked mother?*" Dharma interjected.

"Yes, a visit is of the utmost necessitation," said one of the angels. "She is wicked in her splendor. You know like a gnarly Rider of the Board. Well anyway. Yes, she can tell you all about yourself, David Rainer. She can tell you everything."

The Angel Riders' flaming swords had begun to glow amazingly therein, but henceforth ceased to burn as red and orange and passionate, but now resumed their golden and their glowing hue of warmth. Their robes were glowing everywhere and they were hovering without their boards.

"We are many riders, as you know," the one angel continued, "We are many, now that Maya, you're pure daughter ever purer, resurrected all the lost souls held captive by the Dark Boards. We are ready to provide our services. That pure sentiment is all we want to let you know."

"Thank you angels," Dharma said, waving and bowing.

David Rainer looked on deranged in disbelief.

"What the heck?" David asked.

"Angels are a very different breed," explained Dharma. "They are from the land of non-duality and are very weird. Weirder than the world will ever know."

"Have you met Jesus?" David asked.

"Yes, his quantum field was off the charts," said Dharma. "I have met Jesus and Buddha too. They have great compassion. They delay their own delight for the sake of the suffering, bodhisattvas."

"I knew it!" David said, as he looked aside. "Hey, I was gonna kiss you."

"Yes, well, let's get some rest, and then let's see if you can win me over once again tomorrow," said Dharma.

"What? I can win you over anytime you want," David said.

"Wanna bet?" Dharma said.

"Yeah I do," David said.

Adam suddenly appeared with Maya.

"Hey, mom do you want to bet that an Atlanteans will go to the bathroom first at the committee meeting tomorrow?" Adam asked, as he stepped up to Dharma.

"Yes, exactly something like that actually will happen," Dharma responded. "Now let's just get to bed."

"Okay," Adam said. "Fresh fish sticks tomorrow Queen Ashanti said— for breakfast."

"Adam that is rude to Atlanteans," Dharma answered. "I think she was joking."

The Rainer family then all trailed off to bed.

# Chapter 36

"I will be asking you a series of questions to complete your programming," Synthia said. She is seated on a cliff on a high forest mountain top. She is quizzing he who is covered in black flesh adornments. His mask is black mixed with silver but his retina will never be seen behind the mirrored goggles.

He stared out ahead. He looked up. The clear night sky above him shone with blue and purple shades of space and crisp white stars. He stared ahead again. Over a distant lake there is a thundercloud with lighting striking deep into the water, as well as charging up internally to strike.

"What is your name?" Synthia asked slowly."

The creature looked at Synthia in the only way he knew how to look, sinisterly.

"Hymn," he answered. His voice came from a place that shoots through distance then is nowhere. It was raw and deep like the churning of the earth's intestines.

"Who created you?" Synthia asked. The lightning struck bright behind her.

He looked from Synthia to out among the mountains. "The unknown silent one," Hymn said.

"No," Synthia said. "That is incorrect. It is I who created you."

"You did nothing," said the creature Hymn. "You struck identifiers."

"You are nothing but a collection of commands," yelled Synthia. "And I can put you back within the blackness you came from if we don't get through this programming successfully."

A gust of wind enflamed her hair and lightning struck behind her.

"You know who I am," said Hymn.

"It is you who does not know!" Synthia said. "You are constructed as my faithful consort and together we will end the reign of what is known as earth and start a new planet, for the glory of the unknown silent one."

The creature hovered from his chair lifting it as well along with chains.

"I do know who you are," said Hymn. "You are my Iron Maiden. But you miscalculated in your sorcery preformed to animate my soul. Or, rather, darkness compensated for your shortcomings. Truly, no one made me. I am he, come down into a voice, but I am lightning, I am darkness, I am the wormhole that destroys eternity like a bad spaghetti noodle. I will make worms of existence with you by my side. I am you, but you are my discovery, and I am your creation."

Synthia rose above him in turn. The waters churned and fell from the seas into the sky above the creature into space.

"Thou knows nothing!" Synthia emitted as language through the sound of the flaming rain of dark matter.

"You will sit down in that chair and understand that you are but a proud appendage of my power," Synthia demanded. Then Synthia returned the earth below him and proceeded to dismantle his anatomy with cracks of lava that even he could feel of burning, searing, choking pain.

"I am the mother of the Unknown Silent One!" Synthia screamed. "I am older than the Nano spherules of diamond ice black matter, as the dust of dark creation of creations. I am the transcendent ideology of the pain of Hades. I will have my way. I am the set of all sets."

Hymn broke down on bended knee beneath the pain that cannot be explained beneath the coronary origin of its searing, it's crushing suffocation. He yielded.

Synthia came down from the thunder clouds above them now. She stood before his face because a few steps brought her there.

"Your programming is completed," Synthia said. "Now you are mine. Got it?" She said close in his ear, and quietly, and low, but straining. "No more words and no more thoughts like those. My voice is your command now. My words are your thoughts." She stepped back. "Hit the kill switch."

Hymn went limp.

"Now clean yourself up," Synthia demanded. "We're going into the city in the morning."

# Chapter 37

The rectangle translucent went opaque when Synthia stepped foot inside the transport. Invisible, it tracked across the earth in the early morning desecration, scanning across the surface under a cloaking device, although it scarcely was a necessary option now.

Hymn sat silent now, across the narrow transport from her knees. He too scanned the landscape that was dull and frozen.

Synthia looked back from out the window with an heir of satisfaction, then at Hymn. Then looking back through tinted pane she said, "It's so much easier to think without the noise of life."

Hymn glanced at her for a minute as she sat entranced, almost intoxicated by the desolation.

The world below was in ashes. No city structure had remained. Each passing skyline seemed as though a cloud of metal termites left its buildings broken skeletons. A swarm of locusts desecrated the crops. The smoke lines rose like a giant camp in 1829, or like London during the days of the Industrial Revolution, or like modernity now. The grey smoke, white smoke, black smoke plumes, just froze in the cold December morning like time had frozen solid in its tracks.

Flames and embers remained across the areas. Some of the fire damage had continued burning, because there was nobody to put it out, or care as it spread to fuel or coal in buildings that it could reach. It was left to burn. Some refugee survivors gathered around bin fires where everyone was welcome there.

The world was in a state of pure calamity, apocalypse, and chaos. But the people didn't respond exactly like she thought they would. Instead of fear and murder in this scarcity, in this darkness, they really put their differences aside and came together.

They told stories by the fires, they broke bread, and they shared everything they had. See there are fail safes in their psyche and their DNA, tripwires indicating circumstances where conditioning sluffs off like a second skin, the game is dropped and truth remains an automatic love, just warm and bright.

"Do you see this, Hymn?" Synthia asked. "Do you see what's happening?"

Hymn didn't say a word.

"We have to finish what we started," Synthia said. "They are not as weak as they may seem and it may take a million years but they'll rebuild and build and *why?* To be the same bloody droning fools they are in futures past. What is it with these people? That is why they have to cease to live. I have to save them from themselves."

"Hail," says Hymn.

"You better hail," said Synthia.

"No," said Hymn. Then he urged her outside. "Hail."

Synthia looked outside to find the hailstones falling from the sky. The people ran inside their shanties to take shelter from the hailstones.

"Good, all praise to the wicked spirit of the earth," said Synthia. "I knew the wicked mother would be on my side."

The rectangle descended upon the city in the gloom, entering a thick strip of smog above the ground for fifty to one hundred feet. A hovering ring of noxious dirt and poisonous ammonia strung around the earth and blotted out the sun.

Synthia stepped soft upon the earth. The wind blew trash and litter all around. Hymn kicked a rolling ball of garbage down the street. The odd inhabitants of the town scattered like cockroaches hungry in the grimy sun of frozen winter.

"Let's make this quick," said Synthia. "This isn't quite as pleasant as I thought it'd make me feel."

The hidden people saw the fresh and clean attire of the two outsiders but were too afraid to question anything. Behind a rock they cowered.

The tower of Tomorrow Boards Incorporated now stood in Synthia's midst. Relatively, but not completely left unscathed. The band of neon pink around the rim of cylinder that scrapes the sky was sputtering on and off, twitching, and flitching.

They entered through the double doors. They passed through the mezzanine and then entered through revolving doors. The flood lights were on and fire lights continued flashing. The building is abandoned.

They boarded the elevator working on the generator hooked up to the endless nutrient of Dark Board energy.

"The last of the deposit," Synthia whispered to herself. "Down," she said to Hymn who went to press the lowest button on the panel.

"Lower," Synthia commanded, and opened up a panel down below.

The button pressed, they descend, into the catacombs.

The elevator double doors slid open to a gate. The gate was hinged and Synthia released a robust old and rusty hinge. It shrieked and shuttered aside. They passed into the dripping catacombs of stone. There were flashing strobe lights in the anti-chambers illuminating hieroglyphs in some rooms, codex's in high-relief in others. Ancient aliens in appearance.

"What planet is this from?" Hymn asked, in studying the languages.

"Very ancient aliens from Mars or Venus I compute?" Synthia replied. "Very ancient *natives.*"

But Hymn gave pause while reflecting on the nature and values of the inscriptions.

"Very ancient," said Synthia, and turned around.

"I compute," said Hymn.

They came to the grand dome chamber where our riders led by Dharma flipped the switch.

Synthia examined where the switch exploded leaving marred and mangled ancient rock and metals.

"Exactly as I feared," Synthia said, while standing in contemplation.

"What I do know," said Synthia, after some time. "Is that we need a new switch."

Hymn looked up at Synthia, lifting his jet black countenance; his grill of silver bars caught light from up high within the grand cylinder above the switch.

"There is more that we can do," Synthia said. "I had not considered this before. But this was before that failure of a creature and his pet did not think to stop that little girl and her brother from running round and messing up my plans!"

She, breathed heavily and kicked the ancient stone off into the abyss, and raised high above the shadows of an animatronics man within the reactor.

"I was a fool to try and finesse such an ultimate plan," Synthia confessed. "Not this time my perfect slave of fire power. No, no, no. This time you and I will kill the mouse, with the bazooka." She smashed the rock and it shattered into dust and rain in the catacomb.

Synthia decided to take the fire escape and bid Hymn to man his board after her. Slowly they rose in the ancient nuclear reactor. Synthia rode on her slicing Iron Board. Hymn rode behind her on his board of pure obsidian.

They exited from a distant shaft within a flood overflow irrigation field. Synthia hailed the transport, and the rectangle uncloaked and presented itself before the two who were standing in the field.

Just then, there is was a golden eagle owl of a metallic colored brood of feathers. High above it banked in sensing something with its ancient intuition. Brilliant golden feathers tempered with the age of time caught a glimpse of Halley's Comet in the sunlight and reflected it's rays with its mechanatronic operation in the skies. It swooped low but stayed behind the passing clouds. It's eye actuated indicating that it's honing in on something down below. And in its vision it is noting Synthia below in the city outskirts; with a shadow figure unclear in his animation. The golden eagle owl has a sharper eye than any. It has seen the form within the form of many creatures foreign and local— but this man, who follows Synthia darkly, is a form unknown to the eagle.

The eagle's golden feathers caught the wind and banked and rose again above the smog. It continued climbing until it left the atmosphere. The eagle's metal feathers ceased to nature's chatter. It made a gleaming b-line to an unknown destination, but made a downward, inward angle into the blueness of the earth.

# <u>Act VII</u>

# Chapter 38

The sun rose and gave light beneath the sea. Maya watched as the broad orange circle broke the plane, surrounded by a violet sky adorning all the land beneath in its midst, a royal morning blue. Maya sat upon a melting rock formation holding bended knees before her. Dharma climbed the mountain to her feet and took her place beside her.

"You should always try to watch the sunset... at least once a year," said Maya, smiling.

Dharma smiled back at her.

"That's what Dad always says," Maya said.

"Hmm," said Dharma, with a smirk of morning joy before the world set in motion. "A wise man, that dad of yours." She put her arm around her daughter Maya. "How'd you sleep my dear?"

"As if I laid in clouds," answered Maya.

"Agreed," Dharma said. "There's nothing quite like an Atlantean's slumber."

They scaled the melting mountain down to palace level. The tangerine adornment of the morning sun hung draped on the marbled stones and pillars that were amazingly of a dry appearance in the underground environment. The sun was so clear in the sky that it looked like another planet. The way it was tinted in the water invited everyone to look upon its circle that was almost theoretical in its perfection. They climbed and then rested.

"The food is just amazing momma have a plate," said Adam, rushing up to meet them. His plate was full of shrimp and scallops, seaweed and a grilled anemone.

"Yes, eat, everybody!" said the Sea Queen Ashanti, in her flowing stride. "Trust me, you are gonna wanna fill up while you can on all this fish oil and invertebrate. You'll have the strength of twenty thousand riders."

"Well, you are what you eat," said Tjikko, stuffing his face with lobster.

"Shrimp?" Adam asked. "Where's the octopus?" "I need to grow six arms!"

"Dharma," the Sea Queen said. "After sea brunch, would it be a good time for a deep sea dive? You know... a good adventure for your spirits."

"I believe it would be Queen Ashanti, but not for me, I have decided I will sit this out. A day of rest is on the menu. But, please, take these two and show them everything the land water has to offer."

"Yeah man, take me to your leader, who is the Royal Tour Guide?" Adam asked.

"Umm...," Maya paused. "Okay, sure."

"Great, I'll call the Palace Guide," said the Queen Ashanti. She echoed supersonic hues directed through the water, like that of whale communication. No sooner than she did this, a mighty rider came to her on a board of pearl and coral.

"Dharma, Maya, Adam meet my daughter, Princess Anansi," said Queen Ashanti.

"Hello," Princess Anansi said, softly but swiftly.

"She will take you everywhere you'd wish to go," said Queen Ashanti. "And somewhere you might wish you hadn't. Isn't that right you little puffer fish?"

"It is!" Princess Anansi exclaimed. "I know these waters best of anyone. There's truly nowhere better in the world to ride than here in heavenly Atlantis."

"Yes, that's becoming ever clearer," Adam said, as he introduced himself.

And Maya did the same. "Hi, I'm Maya, don't mind him," she said.

Princess Anansi had a mermaid fin and rode her board by sitting on it. "I turn into an octopus for my spirit animal. What do you turn into?"

"Wolf, me, wolf," Adam answered.

"The Princess hears English perfectly, it's just that when she speaks it, it comes out sort of broken," Queen Ashanti explained. "She has never been above the surface of the water."

"Well, it looks like you three are off to beautifully harmonious times," announced Dharma.

"We will leave you to it," Queen Ashanti added. "Come let's have some mud water while we spa before the second gathering of the boring Board of Boarders."

"Is it boring?" Dharma asked, as they trailed away. "Am I boring? I knew it was too stiff. We should do the second one by fire light with ceremonial drums. Then we'll figure this thing out in no time."

Then the Queen and Dharma passed within the palace walls and disappeared.

"Ready for a ride?" Princess Anansi asked.

"I'll grab my board," said Adam, sprinting. "Finally!" He shouted as he entered a hut.

"I have to grab mine too," said Maya. "But would you like to come?"

"Sure, I love the huts," Princess Anansi answered. "I sleep in them at every chance."

The Princess had hair exactly like her mothers. Her hair was black like squid ink, as it shimmered slowly in the sea looking like it operated in different time zones.

"I like your hair," said Maya, as they trailed off to the hut.

"Your hair is better!" said Princess Anansi. "No one has the golden rays around here. Your hair color is so rare.

The three boarders disappeared in the distance.

# Chapter 39

Adam, Maya and Princess Anansi reappeared among a crest above a hill. They were in a land of rolling planes and blue mountain silhouettes which danced around each other in three shades, just like basic business charts.

The riders three descended a long broad shallow hill into an open plane.

"Welcome to the hills of Alibadún," Princess Anansi said.

"Amazing," Adam drooled, with his mouth agape.

"Save some awe for later, Adam!" Princess Anansi laughed. "We haven't even started yet!"

"Of course, of course," said Adam, recollecting himself.

"Will this ride take very long?" Maya asked. "I don't want to miss a minute of the second phase of the committee meeting."

"Never fear," Princess Anansi said. "I will have you back for your pageantries." She smiled at Maya.

"Hey, I thought you didn't speak good English," Maya said.

"I know more than my mother the Queen admits," Princes Anansi said. "But don't worry, we can take the abbreviated route if you want. We'll be back before you can say 'Anishinaabe, Menominee, and Ojibwa Adventure.'"

"Okay," said Maya, quite relieved but also looking to the side.

The riders crested another hill. A school of fish went shimmering by them. Then a single stingray floated by them.

"But what about the fun?" Princess Anansi asked.

"Hey, yeah," Adam agreed.

Maya gave them a nothing look but listened.

"The wars will come and go," Princess Anansi said. "But riding was the first, and will be the last activity. Am I not right? Why lose sight of what we were created to do? To ride."

Adam put his fist into the air and spun off on his board.

"Because, well, if we lose focus on the war..." Maya started.

"Well, what will happen?" Princess Anansi asked with kind concern. "You might catch an inspiration that breathes into you from a wild ride? And that might jolt your heart and mind onto another track which actually is the track you need to be on just to win the war? Yeah, that wouldn't be so bad now would it?"

Now Maya looked aside again for quite some time. The seascape extended in omnition into nothingness, the great unknown. The mountains and volcanos of the underwater stared her straight between the eyes, while schools of fish did flips as one conducive unit. The circle of life of the sea began to live and breathe, as Maya lived and breathed in the true amusement, the music, the muse of Mother Ocean's secret zone.

"Amazing," Maya said.

"And," Princess Anansi said, as she drew near Maya, "There's even more than meets the eye."

Maya locked into a deeper flow state.

"Oh man," Adam clambered. "Ladies and gentlemen hold on to your boards and boots and hats and even your shorts!"

Princess Anansi smiled.

"We're gonna ride!" Adam yelled.

"Follow me!" Princess Anansi shouted, as she dropped into a water fall beneath the cliff which poured out of a hidden portal.

"What a beautiful environment!" Adam shouted. "Random magic waterfalls from portals!"

"That's the palace sewer drain!" Princess Anansi shouted.

"Regardless!" Adam yelled, as he passed through the downpour.

"Your brothers weird!" Princess Anansi shouted to Maya.

"Yes," Maya answered. "That's why I said 'don't mind him'!"

They rode at eighty-nine degrees, a straight, direct, and downward angle, gaining speed and falling several thousand feet to fields of glowing red orange coral, and luminescent aqua green and blue.

Princess Anansi pulled up slashing coral spray into the air and into two quick turns.

Maya followed by the soaking Adam.

"It's not a race!" Adam shouted.

"It was gonna be a race!" Princess Anansi shouted. "But loser was supposed to swim in dookie and you already did that!"

"Exactly, so it's not a race," stated Adam.

The riders passed into an underwater river valley lined by trees of red orange coral, even with patches of aqua, purple bushes, ancient sea creatures like platypus and alligators, but with gills, that all lined the banks. The tiger sharks appeared in a slither hunt. Then the riders passed into a tunnel where somehow there was a pocket of air beneath in the caves. They raced now even faster through the cells and pillars of eroded rock. Until it funneled into one tight tube. The riders were now on each other's tail like three peas in a pod. It led out into a vortex and then back into a cortex of gravity, adventuring back into the water, into a big old bowl of maelstrom and to a sleeping cracker at the bottom.

"Don't wake Arranticlus!" Princess Anansi warned. "He a grumpy morning person."

They then shot out into an underwater field of great volcanoes. Hundreds of erupting magma pots extending far into the distance.

"This is not what I had in mind when they said we're going on a tour with a Palace Guide!" Maya said.

"I'm the Princess!" Princess Anansi shouted. "I can go anywhere I want! I told you that I know this ocean like the back of every tentacle I have when in my octopus mode. Sitting switch upon her mermaid tail and corral board the princess dodged magma fountains left and right.

Adam looked at Maya. They both smiled with the devilish delight of non-war related life threatening adrenaline rush, so freeing from responsibility.

Soon they entered the moonlit bones of the graveyard zone.

"Watch out for Chupakabras of the sea," Princess Anansi warned. "They feast on broken bones."

"What...how...is this place?" Adam asked, while looking upon the newly rearing moon.

"The moonlit zone is lunar, twenty four hours a day, all year," Princess Anansi answered. "This is where we put our whalebones."

Then they entered into smooth and wild geometric stones of another worldly area. The wide round bowls and spoons within the stone connected and left an opening in a window portal tunnel spoon worm jump track bowl pipe wandering and meandering like a cellular development, but set in stone. Here Princess Anansi flexed in her freestyle moves like Adam and Maya had never seen. They tried their own tricks and went busting off into the sunset that then righted itself when they returned to the mountain coves for kick flips on the coast of cliffs. The trio weaved a web of undulating wave signs, lighting in the glowing coral sticking to their boards. They swerved and intersected and hit each other accidentally, and fell into a field of fire flies beneath a cave.

"Man..." said Adam, out of breath. "Princess Anansi, I am glad you are amazing. Wanna be our friend forever?"

"Yes I do." Princess Anansi replied.

"I forgot what riding for fun had even felt like, for a while," Princess Anansi said, smiling while lying on her back.

"It's like...I constantly forget that." Maya managed to say between her breaths. "I always have to get back to our conflict."

"Always have to get back to the hero game," laughed Adam. "That's the hero oath. Yup. Those is the rules."

"Well, whatever," Princess Anansi said. "Somewhere there is a place, a place that is a time, which is a tranquility oasis. It's it. That is this place."

The three of them relaxed and watched the light take shapes, and bounce off waves, and then break into a firefly parade.

"Princess Anansi, I don't mean to..." Maya started, "I just... will you be joining forces with us for the fight if the time should arise?"

Princess Anansi closed her eyes, then opened them and then looked at Maya. "Our people do not fight," she said.

The three said nothing and sat in silence for a while.

"This is a place where conflict is no longer learned," Princess Anansi said. "A place to aid in conflict resolution and in conferences and such, but beyond that we do not interfere with the surface world or any world that wars against itself, for we are one. This is but a place to wait, and hope for the storm to abate and give way to the calm seas of eternal waters."

"A tranquility oasis," Maya said softly.

Princess Anansi looked Maya in the eye and nodded with understanding.

"Adam and I are young," Maya said. "We are like your babies here. It does not...I cannot even compute or fathom such a peaceful...everlasting..." she said, as her words trailed off.

"Joy," Princess Anansi said. "It is a joy you can't imagine. Yes, but now you know. I believe that I can see we truly know each other's souls. So please, believe me when I say, it is the answer. It all is coming, the day when all the souls, the beings and the creatures in the universe will understand. How can I even reflect this blossom word of understanding out of nothing?" She said, searching.

"Magic?" Adam asked, with the hopeful wonder of a child.

"Miracle?" Maya asked as well.

"Yes!" Princess Anansi answered. "That."

The riders stayed a little while longer in the cave and in the field just playing.

"Well, we should get back to the cabin now, I mean the palace," interrupted Princess Anansi. "Well the cabin is the place I stay in, or the huts, you know those cabins. They're the best. Let's get back then, yes? You're much on time for your committee meeting still.

"Committee, co-schmittee," Maya poo pooed. "You could not have been more right. I can't believe you put me and my brother on this track of inspiration. Thank you, Princess Anansi. We can never thank you enough."

# Chapter 40

The swell of ceremonial drums filed the great hall, arranging rhythms of the hearts and minds of everyone around. The Atlantean's balafons entranced their audience, as they bounced on the rhythm, like lit up rain in lightning.

"You really did it with the ceremonial drums," said Queen Ashanti, leaning down to Dharma.

"Well, maybe we should loosen up a little," Dharma laughed.

Someone swam by handing Maya a maraca and she joined the various maracas gluing all the drums together.

The flags of every realm paraded, as they fluttered in the water. The flutes and horns of conch and coral culminated the crescendo of the symphony. King Swahili sat intoxicated by the quilt of angels with the rhythm of percussion, and the spice of trumpets blazing experimental melodies, or what better would be called the wondrous call of nature. The great sound field extruded through their human instruments but were lost inside the human mind, and redistributed to living nature in its waves and scratches.

Then the Jesters entered in their awkward motions, painted black and white and juggling, and tripping over one another as they tumbled into summersaults and fist fights. If it was planned, the king was not told cuz he was cracking up with laughter.

The Jesters ushered in the circus act behind them of Trapeze Artists and Acrobats and tiger sharks that jumped through fire hoops before the giant sea monkeys who were riding bicycles.

The presentation tapered into a great parade caboose.

The committee of United Riders sat around the jade oval table while the parade vibrated elsewhere. The parades wouldn't stop for quite some time, they had momentum.

Adam moved to join that group, but Maya grabbed him by the collar, and they sat with Princess Anansi as groundlings to the big committee.

"Order, order," said King Swahili. "Let's start with continuing our discussion where we left off yesterday, with the question, 'Is Synthia still alive and still at large'?"

"Without a doubt you're Highness," answered Dharma. "She must be stopped."

"Yes," agreed King Swahili.

"Immediately," said Dharma. "I propose we count our troops, and take stock of all our armies that we have to offer."

The heads around the table nodded in fierce agreement.

"You see, what happened last time, was that Synthia unloaded 7.3 million units of those Hover Boards around the world," Dharma said. "There's nothing on this earth that stands a chance against those numbers."

"It was... dark," Jao Zūn said, recalling the events. "The boards were blocking out the sun where I was, in the jungles in the rainforest of Xishuangbanna."

"Where I was as well," Mercedes Belho said. "They were like locusts. Demons. Maybe there were more than 7 million. Where did she get such an army?"

"Children," Dharma answered. "Kids. From the families of earth."

"Those looked like no kids I've ever seen!" said someone. "They were charcoal black with eyes of red electric embers and some of them had wings!"

"Alright, alright," said King Swahili.

"That is why we need an army of the greatest quantity and quality," said Dharma. "Luckily we found their 'kill switch' this time but I doubt we'll be so lucky again."

"What should we do?" Somebody asked, again. "We don't have those numbers! Should we address the militaries of the earth?"

At this the crowd erupted. Arguments created and discussions bloomed among the tensions of the group.

"I don't think that's a good idea," said Dharma. "Besides, I'll think they'll try their own offense."

"What's left of them at least," said Tjikko.

"Then we have no choice but to enlist the heavens," Mercedes Belho answered.

"You have our Angel Riders at your full disposal," the angel representatives bowed in utility.

"I fear that may not be enough," said Dharma.

"You don't mean..." started an Angel Rider.

Dharma nodded.

"To... disturb... the Celestial Riders... of the extended universe... would be to...," said an Angel Rider.

"We may have no choice," Dharma said.

A long cold silence was then felt around the room.

"Aaaaaah," said the Angel Rider eventually. "Then you may get to find out David's origins after all. We would have to journey to the Holy Mother of All Boards. Yes?"

"Yes, well...," said Dharma, as she looked around to the group. "This is my proposal. You may think on it one night more in this place, but we are running out of time."

"Running out of time?" The Angel Rider's brother questioned Dharma. "Extended riders of celestial bounds? How do you know any of this is true? You defeated her, you killed the switch, and she's gone. How do you know anything at all will happen? Let us wait and see if anything at all will happen."

"It will happen!" Dharma exclaimed, as she stabbed her board into the table sending illuminated rays of ice and snow encircling.

"How do you know?" The Angel Rider asked.

"How do you not?" Dharma opposed.

Zeddefungo entered into the conversation and said, "She is Dharma, Queen of Both Worlds, the oldest sister of the gods. She has had her toes in patterned waters of the fortune since before you walked the infant earth."

"Then she is getting too old for this," said the Angel Rider's Cousin.

"Objection!" King Swahili said. "You're bordering on removal from this city."

"All I'm saying is that when you get to such an age, you might, in your sensitivity, misread a situation, and make it more, make it worse, then it ever was before," replied the Cousin.

The committee members murmured around the room.

"If we don't move now, the earth could be wiped out, again, and maybe for the final time," said Dharma. "Synthia's out there right now, I know it. I know her. I was her..."

Just then something crashed through cathedral window in a portal tunnel in the palace hall. The golden creature fluttered and regained its balance in its hurried flight. It was Ishmael, the golden eagle owl. She landed on Dharma's outstretched arm and started projecting something from her mouth. She opened up her golden beak and everybody watched as she showed the scene of Synthia arriving at her translucent rectangular transport.

Shocked thoughts and whispers passed through the crowds of people like a wave. The Cousin of the Angel Boards looked in astonishment and swallowed his pride with a gulp. Dharma looked on in earnest. Maya looked on in determination. Everybody looked concerned. Suddenly the bird's eye view zoomed in on Hymn in black attire next to Synthia.

"Can you freeze it, Ishmael?" Dharma asked. The golden eagle owl cooed and stopped the film projection. "Zoom in just a little more."

The committee gasped in shock and horror at this man.

"Who is that?" They asked one another. "What is that?"

The golden eagle owl intoned a sequence of coos directed now at Dharma. She listened with intent.

"What'd she say mom?" Maya asked.

Dharma paused. "It is something Ishmael has never seen before," Dharma answered aloud to the group. "Something foreign. Something unnatural. Something dark... something... strong."

"Dharma's right we must move out!" A voice announced. Everybody bellowed.

"Order, order," King Swahili shouted, as he burped and pounded on the table.

"Of course she's right," said Zeddefungo, as he spit at the Cousin's feet. "Shame on you. But let's see what this girls up to along with her new pal in the suit. "Ishmael can you return and get some Intel on their agenda? Any information we can get on what they plan to do will help us out so tremendously and greatly."

"Brrrdthhhooooouuuhhl'l'l'l'l," cooed Ishmael.

"I knew that you could do it buddy!" Zeddefungo let the golden eagle owl loose. "We can count on you! Now fly!"

With the sendoff by Zeddefungo and all of the Board Riders, Ishmael took flight on blue illuminous orthogonal path that were invisible to the nakedness of the eye.

The riders simmered down and simmered out like flames around the fire. They filtered out to places to resume the intermission of their war, to wait, to hope, remaining ever vigilant which wasn't easy, but they waited.

Tensions remained high in Atlantis and the riders tried to keep the balance of their minds while waiting for the weather to clear. Some read books. Some went to shows. Some made games up on their own. Others stayed at home.

"Go and see the Holy Mother of All Boards, David," said the Angel Riders as they passed his way.

Dharma smiled as she walked along with folded arms to hold herself a little. "They're always saying things like that," Dharma told David, as she smiled.

"It's better than their evil cousins," Zeddefungo added, as he walked along.

"Huh?" David asked.

"Sirens." Tjikko answered.

"Ahh," said David. Then he put his arms around Dharma to relieve her from holding of herself to keep her warm.

"You two know all about sirens, don't you?" Ubuntu asked, as she walked with the little group.

Maya, Adam and Princess Anansi followed too.

"What could Synthia be up to?" Maya asked, as she ruminated on her question.

"I don't wanna lose you in this giant war," said Adam to Maya.

"Doubtless she will be back bigger, faster, and stronger," Maya said, with clenched fists.

Princess Anansi looked at Adam. Maya gave pause as she snapped out of her little trance.

"Adam, you will never loose me," Maya said, as she put her arm around his shoulder. "We'll never leave each other's side. I promise."

"Well, that's good enough for me, I guess," said Adam.

# Chapter 41

Synthia smiled madly at her atmosphere outside. "The world is mine," she thought to herself. She smiled proudly at her murdered companion, sitting near her, and awaiting her commands. The sun of blue ice shined into the rectangle as they passed from off the Cape of Good Hope recently, above the southern tip of Africa, and then they crossed a chilling ever freeze increasing ocean into a desolate environment. A desolation evident now and since before the mass extinction recently. The rectangle arrived inside a triangle of longer distance, a harsh environment attachment for the extreme temperature.

"Antarctica," said Hymn perplexed. "What could we possibly be doing here?"

"You'll see, my empty friend," said Synthia. "You'll see." She knelt down in her fluorescent blood red parka, with a hood of forbidden goat hair that was made of self-incendiary thermal heat. She reached down and picked up cold blue jewels of ice and rolled them in her hand. "Old ice, we're close."

"*Old* ice?" Hymn replied. "What the heck you talking about?"

Synthia stopped, turned, face to face with Hymn and said, "I will flip this world on you again."

"I will fight you in your sleep," said Hymn.

"I will haunt your dreams until rebirth emerges in your void soul and re-manifests my form from within you," said Synthia.

Hymn stopped.

"Now follow me you wanker," Synthia said. "We have work to do before we freeze, or worse, somebody finds us."

Synthia walked away, and trudged through the tramping ice and snow beneath her feet.

"I like our little sparring matches," Hymn recited.

"No, Hymn, no," said Synthia.

Hymn followed her into an ice crevasse which slipped into to a system intertwined of crevasses and caves alike. The blue bird skies and sun shined outside, among the shattered blue white ice, floating on the penguin dotted coast that disappeared beneath the concrete ice of caverns, as they trekked down unto the layers of the ancient mystic ice. The earth is ice and they both knew it, but the robot didn't know the depth of their expedition. Not yet. Not fully. They then came to a place in the rock, in the solid concrete water, to a salt corner where the dome had been made by human hands, and amended centuries and centuries ago. There sat in the center pit a well of sorts, of a dark that matched the robots eyes to which Hymn was drawn and mesmerized.

"That is the pit," said Synthia.

"The pit of what?" Hymn asked.

"The pit of our demise," said Synthia.

Hymn stiffened.

"You and I will die down there," Synthia said. "You cannot fathom quite how deep it is."

Hymn looked at Synthia.

"But we will be reborn victorious," Synthia continued. "For thus defines the price to create the strength of the spell, to never be dispelled again. Here, at the world's exit, the grand egress of the earth, we place our switch, of a renewed vow of power. They'll never find it, and they'll never find it twice. If they do they will never break the spell again this time. For because I didn't know, I had no knowledge of those little packrats, when I made the first switch that inhabited the souls of children riding on the great Hover Boards. The demons reigned supreme. The earth was all but ours but then the little Cretans inadvertently were tipped off, but not this time. I'm going to make this spell unbreakable. I'm gonna make this world untraceable, unrealizable and unrecognizable. Until the core of the very universe is shaken in its balance by the desecration of its venerated Saint of the Anima Mundi, the world's soul."

"Thank you," Hymn pronounced.

"Let's descend," Synthia said. She entered certain hand prints in the ice and intonated an incantation.

Suddenly the ice began to melt in certain patterns. In this matter, Synthia revealed a crystal blue control deck solidified beneath the ice. The earth began to rumble in the ice. The tremors of the well produced a transport, cylindrical, that was invisible.

"Inspiring," said Hymn.

They dove in.

Across the world the golden eagle owl, Ishmael was tracking Hymn and Synthia by their spiritual signature in time. Unfortunately she was falling off their trail, within the heart of Africa's dense Congo Jungle.

"Brrrrlld'd'd," cooed Ishmael in consternation. Then suddenly she felt the minute tremor of the earth that she and only some advanced of Anansi's spiders recognized. She regained the trail in recalibrating for the general direction of the tremor from the south. She crossed over Cape Town in the south and saw the trail as clear as day across the Antarctic Ocean. She hesitated, gathered her strength, and then bolted across the ocean leaving a trail of royal blue aligned behind her.

The cylinder descended down the shaft of ice becoming navy blue in age and then it was black. Then Synthia assumed a meditative posture, hovering above the ground, folding her hands, and closing eyes.

Hymn looked outside at the rapidly descending cylinder of blue ice that had turned to black. He gradually lost his point of reference, and his bearings.

"You are gonna wanna make yourself controlled and comfortable," Synthia said. "This is not a short ride." She continued with closed eyes.

"No," said Hymn, while staring out into darkness. "I am home." As they descended into the black, the void of darkness seemed to be impregnated with hues of navy blue and deep of purple, even deeper green but luminous, the three within the void. The hues began to sing to Hymn. An ultraviolet light arrived, a hyper-fuchsia hue, it danced in the absolute abyss. And then the cylinder began to feel cold no longer. Soon it even seemed to begin to heat from his feet up. He imagined a hyper violet growing pink, and then bright, and turning orange and then the cylinder arrived in some space above the vibrant brilliant orange below.

Synthia now opened both of her eyes.

"Is that, the sun?" Hymn asked.

"Don't you know anything?" Synthia snarled. "The core that is the superheated core of earth is not the sun, but it behaves like one, I think."

"Okay," said Hymn.

"But there is a cavern in the rock above the space, above the sun, that sits within the earth," Synthia continued to educate Hymn. "The sun begets an energy of heat and power strong enough to hold a space of air but truly it is pressurized of particles of light. Now, there, above that on the initial layer of the rock, there is a circle of the start and end of all the rock and ice on earth. Its girth is metal at these temperatures and pressure, like a Venus or a Mercury, but Earthen metal never seen or discovered."

She entered the iron concrete cavern and began her way along the platform laid above the core. Then traversed to a peninsula extended in the steel. Then she produced from her pocket a book. She imagined that the platform would produce an iron pedestal of a sullen switch of steel. Lo and behold she intonated and incanted and the switch appeared before them.

Hymn was taken aback.

Synthia smirked at him with a deeply evil glare and said, "That's not even the hard part." She muttered with all her might, and then went into a seizure of activity. Her eyes rolled back, and she was even drooling of her force of magic, in its dark form. Demons reared their shrieking heads, and runes appeared in the air. The very core of the earth was excited, sending a mass coronal ejection that sent them both flying to the ground.

Synthia fell slightly off the edge and hung above the nucleus by her two fingers. Hymn stood above her and deeply contemplated her position. Synthia slipped further, staring at the molten core. She dropped. Hymn caught Synthia before she fell forever to the only thing that really might defeat her darkness of her power.

"I need you Eve," Hymn said, while pulling her above the platform to him. He carried her exhausted body to the transport cylinder and loaded her body on the ship. The transport sucked back up like one of those cool vacuum tubes that are at a drive-thru at the bank. The core of the earth was unstable and shaking, and the shards of steel began to fall onto the transport engine. The transport sped, ascending upward to the surface.

"It was worth it," said Synthia, exhausted on the lap of Hymn. "Trust me."

"I trust you Synthia-Eve," Hymn said.

Ishmael, the golden eagle owl, received the signature of Synthia and the man in black. She traced it across the ice into the caverns, down the frozen tundra of the corridors, and all the way to the Dome of Tabor where the pit of despair remained. She lost what Synthia and Hymn did there. But suddenly a rumble and a sound within the orifice appeared. Ishmael hid away in a crevasse.

Synthia rolled out of the transport onto the solid ice and kissed it. "They'll never find it here," Synthia said. "Never in a million years." She dusted herself off from solidified mercurial shards and balls and shapes that only Mercury could form.

Ishmael oscillated her eye to focus and increase her listening capacity.

"Stop," said Hymn completely frozen.

"What is it? Frostbite?" Synthia asked.

Hymn looked around as if he heard something. Ishmael attempted to make her golden body as invisible as possible.

But Hymn sniffed her out as one of his contemporaries. He had a sense for spirit animatronic animal beings. "There!" He shouted and pointed to Ishmael.

Ishmael fled with all her might to find an outlet in the ice. Hymn grabbed his board and shattered after the bird. Ishmael found a crack and slipped in between for safety. Hymn just bashed through the wall. The chase began beneath the veins of blue ice. They wrapped around the walls and curves of crystal covered catacombs. But she was no match for Hymn and he just tackled her into a plummet burrow and smashed her into the ice. She cooed in defeat.

Eventually Synthia arrived on the scene on her board. "Bring her to me," she said to Hymn.

# Chapter 42

The transport passed over the Southern Ocean, also known as the Antarctic Ocean. Ishmael awakened as the charter made its way for Africa, in the blue-grey distance on the horizon. The blow from being plunged into the crush of solid ice left the golden eagle owl a bit disoriented. Blurrily, she blinked her eyes at Hymn and Synthia. She struggled once but found she was restrained, and anyway there was nowhere else to go.

"So tell me golden bird, I know you're working for those vagabonds that call themselves the good guys, where have they gone?" Synthia asked, as she stood up and walked to look out the window crystal. "What are they up to? Actually, I don't even care." She said, as she walked back to the bird. "I'm more just asking because you had the delicious misfortune of falling into our laps."

Ishmael just slightly rolled her head around her neck.

"Answer me you tin can piece of flying garbage!" Synthia yelled. "Can't you talk?"

"I thought you didn't care," said Ishmael. "Now, can you just drop me off?"

Synthia bit the inside of her lip. "If you don't talk, I'll drop you off and clip your wings. No, I don't care. But I do however need an answer to a question that I asked you." Synthia snapped her fingers to signify Hymn to enter.

Hymn entered wearing black hole goggles and a menace's cage about his mouth. He stepped forward in synthetic flesh, and slithered audibly as he approached. Then he plucked a feather.

Ishmael writhed but only for an instant, holding back a squawk.

"Talk!" Synthia yelled!

Ishmael spit an owl pellet full of fur and skull and wires and steel wool at the feet of Synthia.

Synthia scoffed. She nodded to Hymn. Hymn ripped out seven golden feathers in each of his hands. The golden eagle owl screeched. Still the golden eagle owl released nothing in the realm of information. She hung her head in pained exhaustion.

"Now you've got my curiosity," said Synthia, looking away. Then she rushed toward Ishmael screaming, "Just tell me what you know of Dharma!" She then slammed the golden eagle from its restraints on to its back, and engaged something in the circuitry of the bird. The impact jarred the bird's projector and suddenly the crystal wall was filled with a video that illuminated the United Riders Meeting in a city underwater. Everybody was there and Dharma was giving speeches, leading delegations and the like.

Then Synthia knew everything. Her facial expression took a sinister smirk.

"Good," said Synthia in darkness. "Good. That's exactly what I want to see. It just touches my heart to see them all so worried, so distraught. Thank you Ishmael, I could not have asked for more." She collected herself and stood up. "I was beginning to think that I was gonna waltz right over this dead planet." She stared out the crystal window once again with Africa approaching. Ishmael sat twitching in the corner. The smirk of Synthia returned in all its sinister glory. "Drop the bird off. We have to make another stop."

Hymn picked up the struggling Ishmael, who bit him and beaked with all her strength.

"And Hymn...," said Synthia. "Kill it."

Hymn began to squeeze the bird and started to rip it from its limbs.

From outside the transport came to its final squawk, and then it bombed away, with the blast the doors opened, and the hopeless lifeless bravest spy was dropped deader than a doornail into the sea, some thirty miles south of Africa, below the Cape of Great Hope. So close. But so far away.

# Chapter 43

Back at the palace the sun was setting. The six core riders sat in a rocky out crop cove. It held them like a pocket. All with separate nooks and cranny's that they sat in, as they watched the blood orange sun go down. The tensions were rising. Anxiety was high.

"It isn't like good Ishmael to take so long to return," said Zeddefungo, with trepidation. "She is the fastest bird among the stars. This should have been a cake walk for her."

"I share your sentiments, my brother," Dharma said while staring at the horizon. "And I believe we have to leave first light of morning for the Tree of Trees."

"You can't be serious," said Tjikko. "You heard the angels, you don't wanna open that can of worms."

"We have no choice," said Dharma. "And the angels told us yesterday to go and see the Mother. They're a cryptid bunch. Their code is to live life based on the fabric of empirical truth."

"What?" Ubuntu asked.

"Sorry," Dharma apologized, searching.

Ubuntu held her hands out, appearing to be holding something.

"What is that?" Dharma asked.

"A bucket for your word vomit," said Ubuntu.

Dharma gave her an angry look.

"I'm just teasing," Ubuntu said. "I agree with Dharma. We must leave for Yggdrasil as soon as possible. We either free the beast of the celestial kings and queens, or are threatened to lose the world. And no I do not mean just the earth. I mean the world. The key. You know what I am talking about. These people don't. Some riders don't. They do not fully understand the steaks of this apocalypse. The absolutes may be the only ones who understand. No relative will do," she urged with her heart.

Tjikko looked down and said, "All they can do is agree, and understand that they are wrong." He looked up slowly. "We leave at dawn. Prepare yourselves for the journey of a lifetime. It has been a while since I visited the great realm."

"Is it similar to this?" David asked with sincerity.

"What do you think, David?" Tjikko asked.

David cringed and shrugged.

"No, it's not like anything you've ever seen," said Tjikko.

"Well... that is... similar to this then," David said with trepidation.

"It's nothing like this," Tjikko sighed.

"Where is the Tree of Trees?" Maya asked.

"Tjikko," Zeddefungo said.

"What about him?" David answered in curiosity.

"David, stop," Ubuntu silenced everyone.

David held his arms up in complete confusion.

"Tjikko, David," Tjikko said, "the only way to the Tree of Trees is through the greatest tree of all, called Tjikko.

"That's right," said Maya. "That makes sense. That's why we defended it so dearly, when Radu attacked it."

"Where is this, Tjikko?" David asked preparing to die.

"It's in Sweden, northern Sweden," Zeddefungo answered.

"Right, of course the Tree of Tjikko," David realized. "Fun fact... did you know that it was named by the professor who discovered it, and his dog's was name was Tjikko?"

The group sat dramatically on rock formations as the sun passed down below the sea.

Tjikko spoke, "Fun fact, David, did you know... no it's not? It was not named after some professor's dog or maybe did you know who that professor's dog was named after."

"I think it's just the Swedish name for... tree," said David, cringing."

Adam laughed.

"Yeah, exactly," Tjikko answered. "I am the tree who spoke into the minds of the ancient Swedes."

"Oh, I didn't know that, I just thought the language kind of came about organically and then evolved through practical happenstance," said David.

"Oh good language, David... practical happenstance," Tjikko laughed.

"Some languages... like the Hebrews say the letters are the way the light of God came down in shapes," said David, "... lightning maybe?" He said to himself.

"I'm gonna smack that man," Tjikko said.

"He has a point," said Zeddefungo.

"Guys," said Dharma. "Can you save this triviality for after we attempt to save the universe?"

The riders clambered off the rocks and headed back to the palace. Trailing off the conversation lingered.

"...okay I'll give you that the language is tied to the land, I don't know about the lightning, that's a little crazy," Tjikko said to David.

"Force of nature I don't know why not," said David.

"Shut up and pack your bags, you dolts," Ubuntu ordered tiredly.

Back at the hut Maya knocked on Dharma's doorway. "I wish I was more like Ubuntu, Zeddefungo, Tjikko, Adam, even Dad," she said.

"We all have our functions, we all have our roles," said Dharma sitting down with Maya by her side to comfort her. "I wish I was more like you."

Maya smiled as she looked into her mother's eyes.

"We all have our notes to play within this symphony. That is the divinity of harmony on every level," Dharma answered.

"But will I always have to be the boring hero savior?" Maya asked. "It doesn't make sense."

"Remember what we learned from Jesus that, 'To whom much is given'," Dharma reminded Maya.

"Yes, I remember from Luke, 'much will be required'," answered Maya.

Dharma looked upon her daughter with affinity. "Know, Maya my daughter," Dharma said. "Sometimes this is but a small role of a wave. The role of roles may change in time."

Maya looked at her mother while ruminating on her words.

"Sorry these are large conceptions," Dharma started but lost her point. She readjusted in her seat on the bed of ruffled blankets. "You know the Circle of Life?"

"Like in the lion king?" Maya said.

"Who's the lion king?" Dharma asked.

Maya squinted.

"There is a symphony," continued Dharma. "Within that circle, along that circle. But there also, that circle is a wheel revolving endlessly on course. There are revolving wheels within this circle, but not exactly like a gear, more like a season. More like a year than the seasons orchestrate. The wheel of wheels revolves, and the waves unfold as if there is a sin wave on a sun wave that you zoom in on, and you zoom out of, and the first sin wave was on a sun wave. Two of these things do oscillate between the poles and cycles and swell and increase from two to seven, and zero never meets it's one. The asymptote discovers that it was the line already."

Maya started to pretend that she was reaching for a vomit bowl.

"I have a condition," Dharma mockingly admits. "When you're this old, this experienced, your language will transition from the linear unto the field. Even unto the unspoken. "So, no, in this life, this day of days you may be solid, that is not a problem, you will do the duty of the rock. But the rock will gather moss, and asteroids can be absorbed as granules within the cosmic body of a beautiful creature."

Maya smiled.

"Let me put it this way," Dharma continued, "Your role, which is your position, isn't who you are, you are not the character. You are more the speed at which the character transforms, the rate of change is better to define your soul. So not the rock, but perhaps the speed at which the rock is hurling."

Dharma hugged her daughter. "But forget all that, I'm sorry I am tired and I tend to vomit explanations when I'm tired. You will learn all this in its due course in your unique experiences. The only way. Truly the only way," Dharma smiled. "Besides, you're not a rock to me," she smiled. "I'm iron, steel, frozen stupid broken titanium." She looked her daughter in the eye. "You see, from my point of view you are a simple, silent flower, speaking nothing in the wind as it blows and ruffles you, you dance with joy in its nothingness. I just love you."

Maya quietly prepared the whole night through for tomorrows journey. The hour was drawing near. She felt that she would be tested in the days to come. She felt that the test in truth had already begun. She felt the circles were judgmental in this metaphor. She hoped they judged on the truth within the heart.

They will. She knows it is okay. A song within her heart caught her from within its web and caressed her to sleep. She slipped into unconsciousness and never saw the inflection point upon the $x^3$ parent function.

# Chapter 44

Deep within the Congo jungle, after midnight, Synthia pushed aside a palm fern in the waxy moonlight of the night. Stomping through the undergrowth she trudged, with Hymn behind her, deep into the heart of darkness, deep into the great unknown, the labyrinth of the actual natural world.

"Without the likes of Marcus," Synthia announced, as she hacked and slashed through the undergrowth with her iron edge of the board, "We're going to have to go straight to the source for all our nutrient. And we're gonna need a lot of it."

"Will you let my children ride again?" Hymn asked, as he trudged step by step behind her.

"What is such a question?" said Synthia annoyed. "Of course your spawn will ride again, with vengeance... redoubled in their strength. They will take to the skies like an oil spillage of cataclysmic rapture. But that's not all. When I said kill the mouse with the bazooka, I meant kill the mouse with the bazooka. You will see."

And suddenly the brush cleared aside revealing that they were standing on an airfield level cliff above the largest quarry ever seen. Its glory stretched neigh into eternity. Beneath the moonlight it became a crater of the moon.

There were signs of something working, digging separating layers, but it was not any excavator or any man made operable equipment. This could only be the hand of dark sorcery of beings. The marks were unrecognizable and smooth.

Now Synthia descended into the trench, into the pits of all despair. She fell on twice bended knee and sifted the soil through her hands. There was a tunnel to the right into the rock. She took it. Hymn behind her took in what he was seeing. Suddenly they were in another mineshaft pushing underground. They stepped out in a room of stockpiles, of a glowing natural resource, or was it?

"Start consuming nutrient my little chasm," said Synthia to Hymn. "Fill your dark deep emptiness with power. We are going to need it all!" She screamed and it echoed through the cave into the jungle night.

Extremely close to Synthia the whisper came, "We're bringing it all back home."

# Chapter 45

The start stop button in an F-150 is pressed by Synthia's lizard appendage finger. The engine was orchestrated in the Motor City. Hymn attached himself to the power distribution box from the passenger seat. The car began to go berserk inside by illumination energy of dark electric current that was racing through the screens and doors and wire harnesses. The gentle governed hum of a normal engine rev became a foreign beast of alien intelligence. But then the horror thickened as the two were in the front of one dumb truck with insane energy, the camera zoomed out to the 2030 model year electric F-150, and there it was not one pick up in a garage, but there were actually thirty thousand pickups in a stockpile parking lot outside the assembly plant. Just then all the trucks began to rev and spark with purple blue and black electric light, spreading from the center patient zero to the rest. That's not all, but also... they were transforming into something.

The sole horrific sound, of shrieking crushing metal echoed in the winter concrete night, and was all that was heard.

# ACT VIII

# Chapter 46

In the morning, Maya stood and watched as the conference dissolved, and the mighty leaders said goodbye, to go back to their forces and rally all their troops. The sun was not yet up but everybody was shipping out on the early train, as if the world depended on it. Maya simply stared as the riders filed by and said their goodbyes. She nodded accordingly but, as always, didn't feel in the groove of the occasion. Everyone seemed join into the plan, like little ants marching together. But Maya struggled to join the game of double dutch on this occasion.

Dharma gracefully joined Maya at her side. Her presence grazed Maya's sense of sight and extended feelings. Her touch, its signature, just filled Maya with a sense of comfort, piercing through her early morning angst, and blossoming and blanketing at the same time. Dharma started to speak like a stream aligning, merging with a flowing river.

"What I meant to say, about your role, was that every flower has its season," Dharma said, in soft and reassuring tones. "There is a flower down in Mexico that blooms just once in every twenty-seven years. There is a comet that appears every seventy-sixth years."

Maya smiled, then she looked down at her feet. "I see," she said. "But I still don't like to wait, you know?"

"Well," said Dharma, "patience is a virtue. And you're still my little tulip, soft and velvety, from my perspective."

"Thanks mom," said Maya, blushing at her mother's gushing. "What is Uncle Tjikko from your point of view?"

"Tjikko is like a fine iced purée of poo," Dharma teased, while peering through the group at her brother. "Or like, every color of the rainbow mixed together,"

"Thank you... for that image mother," Maya said, and laughed.

"Get ready," Dharma said. "Let me say my last goodbyes, and then we really should be going." She briskly walked away now and could be seen bowing and hugging, and bowing and hugging. Adam came up from his slumber, yawning, scratching down his bed-head hairdo.

Princess Anansi also wandered over to the two odd riders. "I will see you soon," she said, jesting. "After you vanquish your latest threat."

"What if it gets down here?" Maya asked, worrisomely. "All this fighting. What if the world's cup just overflows? Will there be a battle down here too?"

"Ah," Princess Anansi said. "They cannot reach us here. The heart is not allowed that conquers with all hate and fear. It simply cannot find this place, a heart like that. Don't forget we are not just under the sea," she said, with a wink.

"I love this place," Adam said. He stretched once again and yawned and took in all the underwater metropolis, and all that the surrounding mountain forest had to offer.

"I agree," said Maya. "We'll be seeing you again someday."

"You better!" Princess Anansi said. "You know me... the door is always open. I'll be kicking back in fields of kelp and counting starfish. Comeback anytime."

"I'm going to miss the shrimp," said Adam.

"The shrimp will miss you too, my little friend," Princess Anansi said, as she hugged Adam.

"Why are you hugging me?" Adam asked. "Aren't you going too?"

Maya hugged Princess Anansi goodbye.

"Will you tell the Blessed Mother of All Boards that I miss her?" Princess Anansi asked. "I will visit her in January in the year of Alexzāānder.

"I will tell her that," said Maya. "Whatever it may mean."

Princess Anansi giggled, and said, "Thank you."

Zeddefungo entered with the other riders. "Eight riders, on a mission, hit the road again," he said as they embarked and left the palace gates behind.

"There's only seven of us, Zefu," said Ubuntu.

"Huh?" said Zeddefungo, as he swirled around and rode along and tried to get a head count. "Seven. Well, that changes everything."

The riders drifted along the winding road that brought them near above the hill that marked the distant entrance, of the broad valley.

"So," said Maya. "Now, how do we get all the way to Tjikko from Atlantis?"

"Carefully, and quickly," warned Ubuntu. "I don't like the looks of that new side-kick that Synthia had with her.

"And we'll need to redirect the golden eagle owl, Ishmael to meet us at Nirvana -Yggdrasil," added Dharma.

"The king will redirect her for us, I have already arranged it," Ubuntu added.

"But seriously," Adam posits, "Do we have to fly across the world to get to Tjikko?"

"Of course not," Tjikko answered. "The Lahaina Banyan Tree will transport us to Iceland. It's a hop skip and a jump to Tjikko from there."

"The Lahaina hootey whatty?" asked Adam.

"More like a stone's throw," Zeddefungo interjected.

"It's a sacred tree in the center of Lahaina on the Island of Maui in Hawaii."

"That *did* not make it more clear," David Rainer, intercepted the conversation. "However... did I hear Hawaii? I understand we're near Hawaii but doesn't this road lead to that inter dimensional vertigo inducing water slide that spits us out back into the Bermuda Triangle?"

"That would be right," said Ubuntu. "If this wasn't just a one way non reverse osmosis where it actually allowed us just to float right up above the surface."

"Oh..." said David. "Cool."

"I'm fine with that," said Adam.

"But there will still be inter-dimensional stuff," Ubuntu said.

"Yes," agreed Zeddefungo. "It is, so to say... a bridge of sorts. So there will be trolls.

"Oh, you mean tolls," Ubuntu said. "Like, it's like a toll bridge?"

"No, like, trolls, and I said it's similar to my... said... bridge," Zeddefungo corrected her.

"Oh dear," David said, with panic in his voice.

"It doesn't have a length, it's actually exactly like a... you know what," Zeddefungo said. "Let's just do the egress."

"Do the who gress?" David said, confused.

Zeddefungo shot himself through a sun rise at the perfect point of angle in the sky. The sun was crescent and the riders entered through the moon-sun. So, David Rainer put his arms across his face and braced for the worst. Which is silly, cuz why would he brace for impact with a sun, if anything he should fear the absence of impact which is effervescence, rather it is transubstantiation, or just allowance, or like doorways, portals, gateways, just to permeate which wouldn't warrant crossing of one's arms to brace for impact. Anyways they entered the said sun-moon and made it past the trolls who actually were happy to see anybody righteous passing through this tunnel transport bridge because they hadn't seen a soul in twenty thousand years since the last time.

"Wait, does this mean there is going to be a war?" The trolls were asking each other with a telepathic dimension of communication.

It surpassed documentation that what the riders had to go through, all to bubble up upon the surface of the bottom of the oceans effervesce— oh forget it. Transcendent is transcendent, it's not— really near too remarkable. So there is no doorway that they exited. No, the egress grand was, yes, ephemeral. The bubbles of the riders rose like a carbonation in a soda drink.

Maya stared at Adam through her bubble. Adam laughed and couldn't hear himself so he panicked. Maya laughed and looked upon the approaching surface. The seven riders crested the surface of the waves out somewhere in the Pacific Ocean. They bobbed up and down like yellow buoys in the surf. The bobs disintegrated. The riders' caught their breaths. David Rainer was so dizzy that he vomited in the ocean.

"No more," David Rainer pleaded. "No more." He continued to plead, again and again. "I'll walk. I'll walk from now on." No one paid attention to him.

"We have a war to win," the riders thought, in their minds.

They looked out at the mainland in the distance. It was sunset time in this world of true earth, a portion of the real world. The golden sunset hit upon the island, burning everything a fiery tangerine color of rays on the land and the sand.

Maya zoned into the moment with a look of focus on her face, and treading water she began to swim.

"We ride," said Dharma.

"But the tree is in a populated city," said Ubuntu.

"There is no time for disguises anymore," said Dharma. "Whatever is left of this place, will see us as we are.

The riders then emerged from underwater, splashing vast amounts of water, acting fast to man their boards, as they sped for the coast.

As Dharma had predicted, they arrived within the city limits, and the place was desolate like everybody else. Everybody else. From behind the objects, rubble inhabitants peaked out in fear, understandably, after suffering such a quantity and number of attacks in recent days.

"Help us," cried a little child to Maya, from behind a rock.

"I will help you," Maya offered. "We will help you. We're the good guys."

Then the child ran out to the riders. Maya bent down on her knee and hugged the girl. The child squeezed tight and Maya closed her eyes. A tear squeezed out the sides of Maya's eyes. She opened her eyes. She held the child tight. She looked around at all the devastation and she tried to do what's right. She stood up with the child on her hip and started to speak. "Don't lose hope. I know it looks— Dark," said Maya to the crowd. "You have each other. We have each other. There is something going on that we don't understand. But we can make it through this... I don't mean another... I don't mean back..." Maya looked around. The battered, blistered, dirty people looked at her. "I don't make promises that I can't keep. From what I've seen. I believe we have the answers. There is something coming. Seek shelter. We are gonna end this darkness."

Just then the people urged the riders on in unison. Maya set the little girl down and she immediately ran back to her mother, who gave her a hug and a kiss.

Ubuntu looked at Dharma. Here at this communing of the eyes there came from Dharma, all the fire of her daughter, one and the same. Ubuntu present to her, offering her an inquiry of doubt, a test of certainty for her conviction. Dharma never flinched.

Maya was filled with something no one had seen before. It wasn't hope or courage. It was immaculate purity.

Her brother Adam couldn't believe it but he did believe it. He believed as much as Dharma did. Zeddefungo, Tjikko, David... they believed. As always, even more than ever, they were prepared to sacrifice and trust whatever it would take to win this war. They walked up to the Tjikko Tree together, everybody's eyes met.

"To Iceland?" Maya questioned aloud.

"To Iceland," everybody exclaimed in unison.

# Chapter 47

"It is spreading," said Synthia, behind the jet black glass wall of her forested foothill complex, in the dark.

It was raining heavily. She took a sip of jet black coffee from a chalk white cup. Her job is all but done, and now she must just sit and enjoy the show.

"What will you do with your portion of the earth?" she asked Hymn, who was standing behind her, staring deadly out the window.

"I didn't know that we were getting shares," replied Hymn.

"Hmp," laughed Synthia. "Well, I'm not interested in managing a planet. I'm just ridding it of trash and making sure it stays that way. You can have it all for all I care."

Hymn looked out the window. He was silent for quite some time.

"Then I will raise my children here," Hymn said. "Among the magma and the ashes, as it was in the beginning. Here they can be free to operate in peace, out of the darkness of their hearts, in the regular darkness of the Garden of Eden."

Synthia smiled and sipped her coffee.

"Perfect," Synthia said quietly. "And what of the remaining humans?"

Hymn turned toward Synthia, slightly shocked, and replied, "What kind of question is this?" He turned back to the window. "You know my children need their sustenance. The world order will once again be returned to disharmony."

"Perfect then," said Synthia, as she turned away. "Then all that's left now is to lure out those overlords of the pathetic realms of the Boards Men, pettily protecting helpless humans far too long, like shepherds of sheep." She turned and pounded the window in a fit of rage. "Far too long this parasite has been allowed to wallow and stagnate. We *must* crush this race this instant! Oh, dark lord I cannot wait thus long!" She professed, as the lightning swelled and struck outside, illuminating in the night.

Hymn continued staring out the window through this spike of Synthia's fit. He slightly turned toward her.

"What are you— afraid of?" Hymn asked slowly. "Do you think Dharma is superior? Do you believe the prophecy about her daughter?"

Synthia was motionless and limp, and looked down, with her back turned. The lightning flashed and the lights began to flicker.

"I tire of your weakness," Hymn said. "I can taste your anxiousness from across the room,"

The lightning struck again. The lights went off. The generator engaged, empowering a little flood of red light that dimly and dully lit the room.

"That's why you created me is it not?" Hymn asked Synthia. "And still you have the gall, the weakness to be anxious!"

Synthia turned and her face was dimly, gloomily illuminated red. "What then should I do Great Hymn?" Synthia asked. She stood an inch away from his forehead, breathing nothing.

Hymn stood still, holding fast his heart of darkness. "There is no prophecy I haven't broken," he said.

Upon then the generator started and the light made shapes of angels, maybe demons that lined the room.

"I'm glad that you have spoken," Synthia laughed. "But you still don't know who you have spoken too. Oh, whoops, you must lack that code within your programming. Here, let me load it for you."

Then suddenly the creature Hymn was transported in a solid dream to an ignorant and dimly lit environment, of fire red and dark of night. The blood moon was purely red above him and his mother held him in her arms. It is understood that the time is ancient by the ambience. The creature in the mother's arms is Scarbius, the demonic vanquished mangled soul of evil beings incarnate. The mother buries her face beneath her sullen hood. Her countenance erupted as Synthia's young and demon creature face appeared, in another world, and within another life. The father then embraced him, and Hymn is shown the face of death, it is himself. He is skinned before he was a leather suit. The lightning washed in, and the father and mother of the demon child were relinquished of their child for all eternity.

"It wasn't me," Hymn said, returning to his present state.

Synthia then looked at Hymn, behind his empty lenses. Her countenance beseeched him to understand.

Hymn was horrified. He took a sullen step back, then another.

Then the mother of the demon child appeared and levitated off the ground before him. "I created you, my love, to wake the children," Hymn's mother said to him.

# Chapter 48

The darkness waited inside the mountain, wriggled in the bowels of the earth. Its writing screams could sometimes be described as earthquakes, but it was never really what the energy implied. The earthquake is a mistranslation of the higher frequency and lower frequency of waves outside the visible of spectrum. The ultraviolet lunar waves of Mars in the blood moon gushed out of the demon species hidden in the mountain. Nothing much was felt by the inhabitants of the towns below but Synthia endured their cries. From time to time a child would be drawn into the mountain hills and lost for all eternity. There he then lived with his face among the spirits of the rest, undead, erupting solar flares of dark and pained expressions, luminous blue or indigo in their explosiveness, just waiting to erupt.

Hymn entered into the valley of the frozen ones. He didn't take the podium approach above. He took the ground floor entrance to the chasm of the gulch to greet his children. They all returned to him at once. He stood amid the open floor encircled by the storm of his inheritance. His protocol encompassed the limitations of his soul, but he was unbelievably emotional and powerful all at once. He merged with the souls of the storm. He molded and melded with them in understanding. He meshed with the tendrils in their hopelessness. He opened up his heart. He opened up his mouth to open up the gates of hell upon the earth. He crouched down on bended knee and tucked into a ball. He bent his head into his chest and rectified the lord of evil.

All of the children fell silent. The creatures fell silent. They were in a different place now than the darkness of the cave below the basement. The darkness and the waves of the Purple Ocean swelled and rested before him. He walked upon the water to his daughter. He walked upon the water to his first born son. He drew the legions of his children in the air above the ocean floor of the cosmos, and he spoke one word, into the motor of their souls, "RUN!"

Everything erupted, like everything had once erupted, in the chaos of the dark, the timeless light of good and night engaged, opposed in fight. The seeds of demons flowed inside the portal of the wormhole leading back into the world. The demon spirits chided and bit each other as they approached the glory of the Promised Land.

Hymn rode the wave on his Glory Board, made of obsidian, through the night. The specters watched omnisciently. The deed was done.

The demon children blew the lid off as they poured out like a flaming sword into the night. The lightning swelled and reached a crescendo, intertwining with their flight into the night.

Synthia remained there in the arms of night personified, her consort of the night, her obsidian personified dark matter, interceding. She kissed Hymn while they held each other tight among the gorgeous orchestra of white and jagged lightning strikes in the rain. The cracking, splitting, random paths of chaotic light personified, illuminated the spawn of satan slithering like a snake, into the air from Mount Hood, Oregon.

"I am the unknown silent one," said Hymn, observing the unleashed evil upon the world.

"You are the unknown silent one," Synthia said. "Hymn is the unknown silent one."

# Chapter 49

The seven riders glided on the mist of the end of the evening. One by one they alighted on the ground in the valley where the great, old Tjikko Tree lie.

They humbled themselves as they approached the good tree with honor, from the distance, now walking on foot.

"Good old Tjikko," Adam said, breaking the silence of the riders.

"I can't say it feels so good to be back," said Maya.

"Ah, you just need to make some fonder memories with her," Tjikko argued. "Sure that battle left a bit of a sour taste in our mouths. But as for me it's but a blip upon the endless radar of the happy seas of life with me and the Tjikko Tree."

"That's right," said Maya, in deep thought. "She sure is a lovely tree. And her environment is so aligned with her peaceful humble beauty that it is so unassuming."

"I couldn't agree more, dear Maya, well said," Ubuntu said. She laid an arm around Maya's shoulder, as they walked along together.

Dharma looked up at the stars with a face that was pleased and full of heart. She fell down on one knee reverently and opened up her arms and raised them a bit with her palms up.

Now everyone was taking in the familiar, beautiful and northern air. Even David Rainer was lost in astonishment, with where he was walking.

The sun was fully down. The horizon was a wide and broad and visible at a full 360 degrees around a revolution. Twilight tree tops and the rolling mountain foothills appeared as far as the eye could see. The stars were fully out, yea, but there remained of a ring of putter blue around the bottom of the sky. It looked like the sun was starting to shine on the other side of the earth, and it was casting up a ring of daylight in its absence, then the horizon line was red. The setting sun does paint its red and purple glow, and it grows to the orange of evenings past, and the yellow of the end and middle of the day. And there is perceived a shade of green between the yellow time stamp and that ring of brighter blue below the stars. So the accumulated effect that the riders start to put together is the sun casting the ever knowing rainbow ring around the earth from a red to purple sun, through orange and yellow into green and bluebird colored skies into the night of indigo and violet once again. The shadow of the earth is the stars. The cone of the planets sphere project into space infinitely. A sight to see. A ring and rainbow shadow to behold. The shadow and a planet of the sun begets a rainbow in the stars and all is one.

"Wow," said Maya. "Adam do you see it?"

"I see it Maya," Adam said, without the slightest motion of his open jaw. "I think it means something amazing is going to happen.

"I think you are right," said Dharma, like a fairy godmother.

And before you know it they arrived exactly in the presence of, at the foot of, the good old Tjikko Tree. Tjikko was looking right in their faces.

"Hello, old friend," said Tjikko, bowing.

"Now it is time to travel through a tree like you have never traveled through a tree before," said Dharma to David. "For we are going to a place that before today you've never been."

Maya looked at Adam. Adam looked at Maya. David Rainer stared at Dharma, and then glanced at the tree.

"But I," started David Rainer.

"It's time to find out who you are," said Sophia-Dharma to her husband.

"I've already been so many places that I've never been before," David Rainer said.

"This is different," Dharma said. "This is not a place. Yes, the other places and experiences were admittedly a little bit far out but those were far out in the laws of nature. This is…"

"Non-Euclidean geometry?" David Rainer asked, redoubling his grit.

Maya looked at Adam, and they shared a bit of this possession by the ultimate of great unknowns.

"May the God of Boards be with you," Zeddefungo said, laying a hand on David Rainer's shoulder. "May our soul be permissible in its vision," Zeddefungo finished.

"It is my humble brother, you know it is," said Ubuntu, with one hand on Zeddefungo's shoulder. Ubuntu then laid a hand on Maya. Then Maya laid a hand on Adam. Adam laid a hand on Tjikko. Tjikko laid one hand upon Ubuntu and the other on Dharma. Dharma bowed and turned around becoming transformed into her animal form. Dharma climbed and crawled into the branches of the tree. The other Boards Men followed after her naturally. Maya, Adam, and David exchanged a glance of hesitation, then before they lost their guides they followed after them. Everybody climbed into the tree. Maya could see the tail of Dharma crawling through the branches. Naturally everybody turned into their animal forms automatically. Adam turned into a wolf coyote, and

Zeddefungo too. Ubuntu turned into a leopard. Dharma turned into her snow leopard. Maya morphed into a little snow cub leopard. When David Rainer made his change his children turned around to witness, that he turned into a griffin. Climb they did with all their might upon paws and feathers, as they brushed beneath the mossy boughs and old man's beard of Tjikko's limbs. Ubuntu looked at Dharma with a look of exclamation, and Dharma looked excited too, but in her look there was a hint of understanding.

Further everybody crawled into the branches of the tree and this seemed to go on forever. Maya looked at Adam with a look of wonder.

"How are...," Maya began to say.

"We all climbing so far?" Adam finished her question.

They all climbed like monkeys in the undergrowth, and it was clear between that the intersecting angles of the branches were whisking them away to other worlds. But as they climbed they felt the force of gravity go up and down and sideways, completely gone for now, and then back again.

"We are nearing our escape," called Dharma, from the front.

One by one by one they clawed their way into another place, a separate zone among the rest.

"Welcome to the land of the Creator," said Dharma, as she brushed the brush off herself and returned to human form.

The seven riders crawled between the sticks until their human forms returned as soon as their feet were on the ground.

Maya watched as her feet turned back and she was wearing sneakers again. Underneath them were the cracked dry dirt of desert salt planes with dried up lakes, with cracks forever carved under the bluebird colored sky. Seamless bluebird skies extended immaculately, eternally in all directions. In the distance in the dome above them was the star, too far away to be seen. All they could see was the blemish less blue sky.

"Where's the sun?" Adam asked.

"There's no sun here," Dharma answered. "All is bright."

Adam laughed and looked at Maya, who looked like a kid inside a candy shop, or inside a haunted house.

"For there is no time here," Dharma explained. "The day and night are the same, there is no time. The day is over there, the night is over there. There are no seasons, no cycles, no time. The wheel of life is frozen, shattered, and planted in the ground to grow as trees that feed themselves."

The Tjikko Tree, or at least its replica equivalent, is here amidst the massive desert salt plain in the center, same as the earth, but emptiness surrounds it actually, as far as eye can see. The seven riders stood beside it in the void.

In front of them and deep into the stars there was Zeddefungo.

"Not you Zefu," Ubuntu interrupted.

"Are we dead?" David asked.

"Good question, dad!" Adam said, cheering for him.

"Thank you," David answered, as he smacked hands with Adam's hands.

"Yes," said Dharma.

"What?" Adam asked, cutting his enthusiasm.

"And no," continued Dharma. She smiled. "Consult your mystics on this topic, there's a lot of good books in the field. I especially liked *The True Dharma Eye*."

"I think I read that book, and I actually understand," David answered.

"No you don't get it David," Zeddefungo said.

"Not much of a field," said Adam, as he looked around and kicked a shard of rock. "And I certainly don't see any books."

Maya looked at Dharma with attention.

"No more questions?" Dharma asked. They had none. "Alright, then on we go to Rainbow Bridge."

The riders flew away on their boards.

"The Bifröst?" David wondered. "That kind of Rainbow Bridge?"

"Who *are* you," Zeddefungo questioned as they trailed into the desert distance, an optical illusion heat mirage, of never temperature or not.

"A cheeky piggy," Tjikko slapped him on the back as they slipped out and disappeared into the illusion.

"A griffin," David thought internally.

# Chapter 50

The gravel footprints of the riders bite the loose desert rock as they slow down to a stop. Before them there is, the extending, the burning, the flaming Rainbow Bridge. The bluebird colored skies faded out beside it as it stretched into the distance of the stars.

On either side of the meandering bridge, there is a row of mighty pines. A row along the left edge, a row along the right, guiding like a driveway to the gods in space. The colors burned bright, the bridge waves were like one great ribbon, with the limbs of all the pines it flowed in zero gravity, zero time, and it walked inside one's mind.

The trees returned on either side of two stone pillar gates that marked the entrance of the path.

Maya stepped aside to observe the two, grand, stone columns. They seemed to extend beyond the sky. But where is the sky? She ran her hand along the column with a rounded cylinder base. The stone formed four flat sides but at the bottom of the flats remained a rounded end, as if it were a long and rounded panel, like a park ski, or a snowboard. There was a rounded tip at every panel side, all four ends. She looked across unto the other gate. She ran her hand along the panel, crossing the space. The trees extended behind the gates in rows. She took a look down the burning flaming Rainbow Bridge. It seemed to stretch for countless miles, moving, like a snake, or like a ribbon.

"This is familiar," said Maya.

The group stood quiet in her reverie.

"This is not like I'm returning, this is just familiar, almost like it is in me," Maya said, looking at Dharma.

Dharma wore a face of delicate understanding. "You are... Maya," Dharma said, eventually.

Maya stared without really looking.

"The space you have just crossed between the gates, the line you have just made before the Rainbow Bridge... that line is... you."

"I... I don't understand," said Maya.

David looked at her with love, but didn't know what was happening. Maya's eyes met his normal eyes.

"Maya is the line between the one and two, the chaos and the order, sort of like light and dark," Dharma explained. "It is best described as differentiated... and undifferentiated." Dharma drew a line upon the sand. "On this side is the one, the non-duality, the chaos, the void, she that is undifferentiated. On this other side is the manifestation of *all* that is. Represented by the pure white light that manifests the seven colors of the rainbow."

Maya's eyes became wild with illumination.

"And that is just the tip of the iceberg," Ubuntu added. "All of nature, all of existence, is on this side. Think of it. Does it seem unbalanced? It isn't."

"It is wild," Maya said, with a smile.

"It is wild," said Ubuntu, in agreement. "Maya is the balance."

"Wild," Adam added, in awe and wonder.

"But I'm... just a person... just a girl," Maya said, confused.

"Indeed, but you are more than that," said Dharma. "It's like I'm always telling you that you are like the pattern of a comet in the stars that winds its way mathematically through the solar system, aligning everything within its path. You... are the solution."

"But," said Maya.

"No buts," said Dharma, smiling. She put an arm around her daughter, as the riders faced down toward the fated Rainbow Bridge.

"Come, there's more I want to show you," said Dharma. She crossed through the gates to where the rainbow met the edge of earth.

"How do you... how does this one work?" David asked.

"This one?" Dharma said, as she looked back, as she skated on her board. "This one you just ride, like ice... like fire."

Everybody joined her. David first. Then Zeddefungo surfed the flames a little. Soon the group was cruising slowly between the trees. Adam did a kick flip.

"This is great!" Adam called out. "We should have one of these in our kitchen."

Maya squinted at him in her weird way. But then she laughed and carved a turn.

Tjikko ran a hand along the line of boughs that felt angelic in their fir.

Everybody floated into the great unknown in what seemed to be forever. This thing was hitting different. The kids were like watercolor paints. The angel saints appeared within the mold. They floated over like whales. They sailed into the great unknown. The seven riders were red, orange and yellow. Then the seven riders were green, blue and indigo. Seven riders. Violet. The Milky Way was like the paint of the page master, pouring and swirling in the miasma of the maelstrom of the mermaids, with their wings their songs merged and molded with the palpable orchestra of colors. The grand, grand auditorium awaited. Before them were the final gates, the brightest light of white spaceships, stars, and outside. The color tour closed, with majestic, silk and goo like tie dye. Then the light became transmogrified. The flight of riders were suspended in a grand and great white chasm of the light. Maya shielded her eyes. Adam shielded his eyes. The light became a storefront, or a weird inside-outside arrangement of a palisade within a place. White was the face of the walls, white were the windows, white were the halls of the archways that led into a center for performing arts. White were the stairs that they all stepped on without making a sound. Adam stomped and there was no sound. Silently they passed into the hallway. They walked down the whitest lines and shadows with no lights, and the shadows were in unreal locations. Maya walked and quietly pondered what she was seeing.

They reached the final room. The insanely large location gave way to the greatest hall of all. The hall of halls. There was a ball is in the center of the hall. The ball was white, and whiter than white. It was alive. Illuminated it alighted above them nobly fixed, floating around on open space, it rested, it said it's sequences of something up around it, like a Ring of Saturn or a solar flat but nothing understandable to the riders. It was something. Its language could be seen. The seven riders stared and circled the ball carefully. The orb imagined everything. Surprisingly, the riders could hear each other, somehow. The ball was the frozen sun. The Arctic Sun illuminated white. The sequences and patterns swirled around like cycles, in and out. David cried as he looked at it.

"Time to find out who you are," imagined Dharma, to David. David could hear what she imagined.

Then David looked. The ball was glowing, dropping, snowing souls and information to the snowy ocean underneath. Something seemed to be beneath but looked like a hole that had not reached differentiation. Maya understood.

"Is this...," imagined Adam, to David and Maya at once.

"The Tree of Trees," imagined Dharma. "The Tree of Life, of life and of death. This is the Mother of Boards. The tree which, when it's leaves are falling pours a soul into the world. The tree of which, the final souls are falling. But the Tree of Life...," imagined David.

"It's all trees," imagined Ubuntu.

"It's the sun," imagined Dharma.

"It's the moon," imagined Ubuntu.

"It's the rain," imagined Zeddefungo.

"It's the rock that falls," imagined Tjikko.

"It is the roots," said Dharma as she placed her hands on Maya's head. "The red and blue. The two to make the one. The 23, the 24, the 3, the 7, 12, 11. You are Maya Rainer. Sophia Rainer is your mother. Dharma and Sophia Rainer are the same."

The orb opened. "David, come to me, my son," said the orb. David looked at Dharma. Tjikko, Ubuntu, Zeddefungo, Maya, Adam came to David. David came with them to Dharma. "You are David Rainer. David Ardefiel, my little angel," said the orb. "David, you are the man in the moon," the orb continued. David looked at Zeddefungo. Zeddefungo cracked up laughing, without holding back.

"Your brother is the howl that you cast upon the lunar surface, Zeddefungo," said the orb. "You have a mansion," the orb told David. "You have an angel race within you. You are real. Remember who you are."

Then David had a revelation. He suddenly was floating in the room. The people came to him as memories, the souls and all the kings people passed through his form, and put him back together once more. His eyes changed. His eyes turned white and he remembered.

Zeddefungo remembered too.

David Ardefiel remembered that his wife Sophia Dharma slept in peace within his arms upon the moon. Their children woke for lunar Christmas and the angels in the 28 of mansions rose and held their coffee.

"That was long ago," said David.

"Ardefiel, Ardefiel," said Dharma wavering, hugging him while crying and quivering. "Sophia Dharma," David wrangled and remembered. "Our children." He saw Maya in a different and eternal light. He saw Adam in eternal light. They came to him. He rejoiced in the midst of the coming orb. White, everybody's clothes had turned to white.

"*I* am the man in the moon," said Ardefiel.

"*You* are the man in the moon," said Dharma. "*He* is the man in the moon.

# Chapter 51

"We are here to petition you to give us aid," Dharma said to the Mother of Boards.

The Tree of Trees, the Güf, the world tree beyond all concepts, became a woman, took a woman's form and walked out of the orb into the room. She was the Mother of Boards, and no one remaining was shocked at this transformation. They were there to ask her for a winner.

Adam walked up to the Mother of Boards and he hugged her at the waist. She loved him. She embraced him and picked him up, and put him on her hip like he was a baby.

"I love you," Adam told her.

The light formed smiles. Her amazing hair waved in the space like a fish's fins, like an ocean, like white lave. White lava is beautiful and perfect. She was every form. She was your form. She was the one. She reigns. She lives in you.

Still holding Adam in her arms she intonated, "I am here to give you strength."

No one spoke. They knew that she knew exactly what they needed.

"You are here," said the Mother of Boards. "You know the cause and effect relationship of this decision. I will give you this as if it was a Letter of the Law. For that is what it is. Now come."

She led them to a white table inside another giant room. The chairs were upholstered thrones of white that surrounded the table. Several paintings that were white beyond our concept lined the walls. There was no ceiling. Black space lined the sky with dusty white stars. We are not here. There isn't anything or nothing taking place in this arena that the woman of the globe would sit in at the table, and everything was happening in and out of time.

The riders all understood.

"Cake?" Mother of Boards asked the riders. She, the lady, offered them cake as she cut a slice of an immaculate white desert before their eyes. "You know that when celestials appear undifferentiated they are fine, but when they manifest in solid ice they get a little weary, and wild. Yes, all is bright," she said wildly, beaming like a Princess. "All is bright when they play their part. We win the game, there are no answers here. Now, step into the place of paradise."

The riders walked outside behind the lady. They were led to the white steps beneath the balcony of white that led outside.

Outside the land was green. The people were gathered in a park with a river flowing through it, and the sun was golden, and there was a Dog and Pony Show, and there were picnic blankets on the ground, and people having a barbecue, and ladies visiting on picnic benches, and five thousand people being fed by Jesus. Jesus bowed to the Mother of Boards as she passed by him.

"Where is Father Gravity?" Dharma blurted. "Father Electricity?"

"Beyond," said the lady. "He is beyond. He is Him. He is surfing in the swell of indifference, in vortexes of differentiated waves of divination, in the zone of heavy beautiful amazing un-differentiation. I will join him shortly. Come." She led them down the steps into the garden. Then down through all the people. It seemed like only 20 million souls but it was uncountable infinity. "The others of uncountable infinity are in the peaceful valley, listening to rain." She was still carrying Adam on her hip.

"What are we doing?" asked Maya. "It all makes sense. I know. We reek. The war will come. The war is me. The tree is an illusion of a sea of never dying babies, that I don't know if it's a flower growing or a game."

"You are getting it," said the lady. "The sleep of sleep is life. Or solid. We are cake, and we are here eternally. Here is just a place right on your map. There is just a place right on your map. War is just a place right in your map. The world is the world. The stars, the world, the time is the place. There is freedom. There is Jesus. There is God. There is Mary. There is joy, and there is meaning. I will see and gather the deceased ones. People are souls. Where they are on a map is revealed. We are here forever. There will be time. I promise."

Maya smiled.

"I don't know how to tell you, the ironing out, and the figuring out, it is simple, it is weird, it is the grinder, and maybe it's the motor," said the lady. "It is all your language...of the lost. Yours will be time... for everything... for everything. For time forever is not ending... is not ending. Time for endless fear to go flat. Time for everything to go flat, time for everything to show you what I made you. Time for joy. Time for love. Time for everyone to wake up and become a scientist and do the math on a big computer just to bring you back... and that's... nothing. Time will be okay."

The sun set on the people and another sun came up.

"Infinite," the lady said, turning to Dharma. "A simple word, your earth actually doesn't understand. For if it did, there would be love."

"Take your angels, take your saints, and bring me back my babies," said Dharma.

# Chapter 52

The earth was dark. The night was upon it. The golden eagle owl laid in shambles at the bottom of the ocean. The ocean was midnight blue. The waves scratched back and forth, with no crest. Beneath the immensity of water laid the golden eagle owl, Ishmael in the sand. The moonlight tried with all its might to shine upon her but it couldn't reach her. She was in the dark, in the crust, in the sand. The sand washed over her with the rising, and falling of the tide. She closed her eyes, or her eyes were shut. For there she laid for three days straight without a sound, without a hint of life. The lightning flashed up above. She was somewhere off the southern coast of Africa, where Synthia and Hymn dumped and abandoned her, and juiced her for her final worth.

But then... there is a spark. There is something in the pile of the rubble of the ashes that she laid... inside her something bubbled, like the pattern of her life force had not stopped. Something twitched, even if it couldn't be seen for its subtle animation, it could be heard. A school of fish twitched in its little nick and knack that came from being buried in the sand. The clicking echoed through the liquid of the currents. The school of fish swim by each way and twitched this and that as the clicking loudened. The shambles and the ashes animated. The water started to swirl about the animal. The creature stirred and blinked and its eyes actuated their retinal abilities. Suddenly the water swirled into a gnarly storm beneath the sea. Like a cyclone rushing in a turbulent amount of leveled flow. The golden eagle owl went invisible again. But the storm kept rising from the deeps. The levitating orb arose slowly from the ocean. Suddenly the torrent stream of rushing orbital rapids were ignited. The ball of water became a blazing ball of flame. The ocean spread away from surface to the depths. The fireball enlarged shedding water clear in every direction for a seven hundred meter circle. The bird appeared. A phoenix in the flame emerged in the darkness of the night and stood amid the midnight water blue which shot her up in a wall around her. On fire, she walked toward the shore with wings bared wide. As she approached land in South Africa, she pushed water like a goddess. Ishmael had taken the flaming form of a phoenix, and she leapt upon the runway of the ocean floor. She jumped and leapt and ran, with her stride increasing till she reached land and she took flight.

She hovered and ascended to 20,000 feet above the sky. Then what did she see? The earth had become a shroud of darkness, and chaos was consuming the earth. Everywhere for miles in the distance to the curvature of earth the flaming bird observed the slaughter of the planet by savages on boards that were of black charcoal skin and flaming eyes. Their wings of ashes sputtered embers in the chaotic path of devastation. The end of the world was near.

The bird observed the slaughter, as it hovered and articulated, with its red wings enflamed. It hesitated its flapping, then dropped several feet, then flashed to the surface like a fire breathing dragon in search of the cause, the information. The bird observed the demon seeds as fine as sugar, like a million schools of devil fish swimming in the skies like termites. Then, in the ground she saw the oddest most troubling information she had ever seen. Suddenly, a mangled automotive vehicle, that was bright from within with purple violet lights that were like a dark electric matter, burning in its core, took another car and touched it, and the later animated and crushed itself into a creature, like a greasy sheet of tin foil. The phoenix Ishmael, casted back in horror, and gasped. The automotive armies all across the land was possessed, and marched forward spreading some apocalypses disease to every auto... every airplane... every steam engine... and every heavy hard machinery, and into all other worldly armies. The beasts, the pests, the catatonic pandemonium of the savages, and mechanatronic satan seed machines were eating the earth like it was a piece of cake. The phoenix flew up to the hemisphere where she could see both the destruction and the spreading of the machines' disease upon the earth that looked like glowing lichen on the globe of doom.

Ishmael redoubled herself, regained her courage and composure, and with all the speed of a phoenix in her new found form, she rushed to the Tjikko lighting Rainbow Bridge. She was like the fire of a shooting star at light speed. Her orthogonal trail of orange enflamed the lightning sky.

# Chapter 53

"Are you my grandma?" Adam asked, still on the hip of the lady.

"Yes," she said. "I am Leila."

David Ardefiel was taking laps around the sky in his new griffin form.

Maya smiled lovingly upon her father. She remembered that he remembered that he is a famous angel, as he soared above the immortal golden rosy world of populated heaven.

"I *knew* he looked familiar," said Tjikko, admiring the flying griffin, lunar angel in his midst.

"The prodigal son has returned," admired Zeddefungo. "You know where to find me after this whole world destruction thing blows over."

"Where? Mars?" Ubuntu asked.

"That mansion on the moon pool, obviously! That thing has been abandoned for a hot eternity," he answered curtly.

Ubuntu shook her head. She moseyed over to her sister Dharma who was standing in the golden sun observing all the paradise that was taking place.

"This place really cast a spell on you," said Dharma, sensing her sister Boonty walking up to her.

"It sure has," Boonty mentioned, dreamily.

"But we have to get back to the others who are mobilizing," said Dharma, somewhat snapping out of it. "I fear it might already be too late."

"No, you don't," Ubuntu smiled dreamily, apparently remaining under every spell.

"No... I don't," arranged Dharma. "But regardless, nonetheless..."

Suddenly a flaming bird appeared and all were taken aback. "It is worse than we all thought," the flaming melting golden bird imbued.

"Excuse me," Zeddefungo mused. "Do we know you?"

"It is I, the golden eagle owl Ishmael, in phoenix form," Ishmael said. "The evil Synthia had smashed me out and cast me down into the waves from on high. I reemerged a couple minutes back and saw an absolutely horrifying scene."

"Ishmael!" Ubuntu rushed to her aid. The phoenix collapsed in her arms.

"Fear the worst," the phoenix squawked. "Fear the worst!"

The Mother of Boards recovered from her memory the images that Ishmael had come to pass on to the riders. They laid her burning feathers on a healing bed inside the whitest house. Maya looked upon the bird, who was in bad condition, with a sympathy unrivaled by her peers.

"She is pure, the light of love", Maya said. The phoenix laid her wing in Maya's arms.

"Take us to your angels," said Dharma to the Mother of Boards.

They climbed aboard a transport that took them through the cumuli clouds that looked like a universe in grandeur. Arriving at the Place of Angels, the Holy Mother gave pause.

"Protect her," Leila said to a girl.

"Maya is the reason we are here," Leila said. "She needs to be... you are Dharma. I'm am the Mother of All Boards. We are not going to let another bad thing happen to them."

"I am her Dharma," responded Dharma. "We are."

"Here is your artillery," the girl announced.

Now the gates opened to a rosy clouded dome of light and chaos, where the angels walked and rode the skies, and played for all eternity. They fought, they wrestled, and harmonized angelic choruses beyond the ear of humans, that the radio spectrum, never touches. Never have any come out from off the walls of this enclosure for an eightfold ancient period. They sleep with wings immaculate and hang upside down like angel birdy batts. They hum and line the wall like bees. They have pretty faces, beasts and angels that they are, for they were created just to fight the demons that will fall. The dragons they will battle. They shrieked as they streamed across the face of Dharma.

"*Silence!*" Dharma echoed bravely.

The holy city had endless atriums and villages and angels writing poems by the fountain side, and cream white masonry abounding in the endless halls and mazes of the crazy sky birds.

"Hi Dharma," said the Twin Angels from the conference, as they flew by. "Can we help you?"

Dharma looked obliterated. "Yes, you can, there is a war remember?"

"The war is over is it not?" One Twin Angel asked.

"No, it is actually about to start," said Dharma.

"I'm sorry my amalgams are all mixed up," said the other Twin Angel. "I mean my algorithm. Maxfiel is yours."

"The war! The war!" Maxfiel said, after being awakened from ancient slumber by the banging angle heads against his bed."

"Yes, his algorithm is mixed up as well," the other Twin Angel intoned.

"It's time to win the war!" Dharma declared. "It's time to save the world. It's time to pull the plug. The time is nigh. The prophecy is here. The final soul leaf has fallen from the Güf tree. Leila saw it yesterday and didn't think that I had noticed. The time is right. It... is...time!"

"What is time really?" Maxfiel engaged from the atrium.

Dharma stared ahead, with a full head of steam. She hesitated and lost her focus for a moment.

"Angels!" Leila commanded, staring ahead.

The Angel Battalion gathered in the peaceful valley. The legions endlessly fluttered in a weightless drift.

"But how will we get all the angels through that little hole of the Tjikko branches?" Adam ruminated.

Everyone came to a stop.

"Yeah, that is actually one very, very, very good kind of a question," Zeddefungo added. "How will we get them through the tree quickly, oh great Dharma, oh great Leila, anybody?"

David stepped up from the back in griffin form. "I believe that I..."

"David, psssst," Ubuntu whispered loudly, bringing all that he was doing to a halt. "You..." she signaled him to sit down with her hands.

"I believe that I...," David tried to continue. "What?"

"Your still in griffin form," said Zeddefungo, laughing.

"It doesn't matter," David argued childishly. "Oh fine, alright okay."

He switched back to human form from griffin form. He opened up his mouth and raised up his hand. But then he switched back that instant and announced in his griffin form with power, "I believe that I could be of some assistance on that account!"

The Lunar Angel faded into the angel hordes and greeted them all, like a long lost friends. "I have a plan," he said. "Let's kick some demon baby skinny butt!"

They all fist bumped each other in agreement.

# <u>Act IX</u>

# Chapter 54

The sky was silver. The rust of the oxidization of war hung in the air like paint, like magic, unnatural. The sun could be seen as only a white circle behind it all. Its rays were stripped bare, but its bare disc of light remained a flat curiosity.

Below each setting sun there was a winding line of stiff necked passengers, wrought and bent with strife, leading to regional stock piles of the Tomorrow Boards that took possession of their sons and daughters, burning in the silver sun. Mounds of burning boards had spread around the world. The downcast inhabitants of earth had come from miles around to line up and dispose of and destroy the talismans, the obelisks that took their children's souls. The children laid at home in other heaps of rubble, their makeshift homes, nomadic like, in migrating rubble. They shivered under terry cloth rags. The smoke stood up like steam from every mound across the land, and the face of the earth.

The people were defeated. They had no hope of fighting back. Their armies were reduced to nothingness and scraped by automotive monsters in the millions, that wreaked havoc from Alaska to Brazil, the Kremlin to the Cape of Good Hope, and to all the lands of the rising sun.

On the other side of the world there was no silver sun. There were only blood red moons and billowing cumulonimbus clouds passing by and reaching high into the sky, edged by plumes of moonlight blue. Below its mounds burned the Tomorrow Boards, a curse upon this land. The fires lit the night. The winding lines of people remained from day. The children shivered and quaked in their sleep, in the dark.

The battle outside raged. Mercedes Belho and her team of Rain Forest Riders barely held the line inside the Amazon River basin during the night. These automotive giants were a force upon the land. They tagged each other and transformed into sorcerous purple shockwaves from the nutrient. They crushed like recycled pop can garbage, into bipedal format of one and two ton demons with the speed of roughly a hundred horses at their feet, and with only malice motivating them.

Synthia stood with Hymn upon the highest level of her tower. There beneath the glowing neon pink illumined beacon, her demonic lighthouse, she orchestrated the Armageddon, like some ultimatum warden of the end of the world. They just stood there in tandem in a stance with outspread legs. The tower penetrated the storm clouds of the night. The blood red moon was drowned in smoke.

The riders of the Midwest came down from the north hills and rivers. The spirits of the valley rose and came out of the woodwork to the front lines, to defend the world in the final stand.

The fighting took place at the ground floor of the tower and extended outward in a radius of blood and carnage, extending to Chicago and New York, as the epicenter continued to extend. The fighting in America was one sided. Their patron Zeddefungo was missing in action, so the rogue and rusty armies did their best to defend the land. Again they fought those who threatened their homes. The common man and woman watched from the shambles and were amazed to see the ancient warriors of the Cherokee, Lakota, Ojibwa,

Apache, Navajo, and Sioux fight as if they had never left this world. They were far wiser than the invaders. They returned to their home land, knowing this day would come. The men and woman pointed at the ancient warriors, as the war dogs hovered. The warrior tribal screams united them in their common goal, to defeat the machines, using their natural ways of fighting.

In Alaska, Bullet Eyes and the Man of the Mountain were in charge of every mystic person who was native, peaceful, loving, natural, harmonious, crazed, or beautiful. They all fought and they all fell. They fell like a Great Oak in the forest, and like a Red Wood Tree on the Pacific Coast, and like the Great Sequoias too. They drove the invaders to the sea.

Jao Zūn and his armies crumbled.

"Just look at their numbers," Jao Zūn said, with wonder. "We are not fit to win this battle."

"Jao Zūn!" Cho said. "You are no general if you think that way."

Of course, Cho is ignorant in the face of what they both see. As far as the eye can see, as far as life is itself, increasing at the horizon and extending into infinity these metal monsters raged like nothing, nothing anyone has ever seen. In the lands where no one fights back, there is absolute demolishment. A plowing of the earth. A sowing of the sinister seed that brings in the apocalypse.

Just then the lines of men and women are shocked to see the flaming mounds before them turn to a neon violet flame. Everywhere on earth the pylons light up violet, one by one. Suddenly the shaking children are pulled by something from their huts. Screaming they are dragged out into the air of night and silver of day, depending on the hemisphere. With looks of shock and horror on their faces they are levitated toward the pylons. Suddenly the piles of the burning Hover Boards burst forth extruding all boards outward. Floating in the air they draw their linked children to them. Simultaneously the spirits and the demons that erupted from the mountain in the night, reached their unknowing victims, and in one coordinated motion a child, a board and a demon are fused together once again. Their nightmare returned.

Synthia and Hymn witnessed their orchestrated vortex, and coordinated doom impending attacks.

"I love it when a good plan comes together," Synthia expressed.

"A true masterpiece to behold, my love," said Hymn, adorning her with praise.

Synthia strolled lacksidaisically to her throne, which was a big executive equipment leather armchair, seated at the head of one extremely large, executive equipment oval oak mahogany tarantula obsidian table, that sat on the top floor in a glass cage on an iron tower, swaying in the storm clouds brewing in the wind. "Out with the old and in with the new," she announced.

She plugged a Bluetooth USB into the socket in her hip. She brushed back her flaming red hair and dimmed the lights. A projection from her head appeared connected to the atmosphere, the environment, any GPS location she imagined triangulated, by the seismic reading of electric signals running through the millimeters, nanometers of the surface of the earth. It displayed exploded views of figures fighting, animated all in real time with detailed views.

"They said I was the lowest of the Dark Boards. They said my plan was weak, and inconsequential." Synthia sits and spins in a quarter circle, staring at the views of war that cycle through. "I say I play the long game," she scoffed. "Where are they now?" She posits. Irrelevant!"

"Hmm," said Hymn, attentively.

"Not only that," continued Synthia, "But they are long extinct. Absolutely nowhere to be found." She stood up. "And where am I?" She sat down and issued quietly, "I'm in the ivory tower." Outside lightning struck, without the rain. "No one said goodbye to me. There was no one left to know there was additional hope in me. The ship had fully sunk and eons later, from the wreckage, the game was over, I emerged victorious!" She extended her fist and slammed it on the hardwood. "Are we even loyal to the ancient cause?" Synthia asked, in revelation. She turned a full 180 revolution and faced Hymn. "We... we could start a *new* cause. We are not loyal to the death and the decay of what was once a sorry organization. We won't have a name, we won't have an institution, and we will be untouchable... unstoppable. Yes, the plan was like this all along, I just didn't see it sitting in the recess of the outline. First, earth. Further... everything. I was never one for every way the Dark Boards operated, I just never knew, that's 'cuz I was created at the bottom of the next ascended level... not the bottom of their lower frequency." Synthia continued brooding, fuming back and forth across the room.

"Come, Hymn, with me and join me, we will control the universe. Our order will surpass the boundaries of existence and our glory will be infinite until the end of days," Synthia said. She stood up and continued, "Which will only end because we order them to end. Let us squash this simpering fire, let us extinguish this flickering flame." She turned to Hymn, ending with, "Let the riders of the light come as they may. I am on a tidal wave of pure destruction!"

The demon children minions streaked across the gleaming iron sky of brooding neon orange of night, as if the fighting took place in Japan or Patagonia. Across the land the Ancient Natives on their boards unleashed the wildest attacks of old. Below the charcoal minions dragged blackened ash, stainless steel, and aluminum, while the iron giants shook the earth with great stampedes. The view of night looked like a rainbow of the riders of the lights, attacking against the evil, and the anger of the purple and the red illuminating blood, and psychic operations.

"I can't hold them back!" Mercedes Belho cried in the Alpines, and leaned into a beaming oval shaped attack of iridescent pinkish red energy. The energy whipped through scores of automotive robots, while doing minor damage to the numbers. But the damage that was done to the energy of Belho was the greater of the two.

It is no different in the Asian quarter. Jao Zūn was running out of steam. He summoned up an ancient character attack which was very taxing on the spirit to enact. The glowing characters emerged like a glowing horse herd stampeding through the crowds of Dark Boards or whatever entity they called themselves these days.

The warriors of the Tree of Life launched their attack amidst the runs and shrubs of ravaged jungle forest fires, wildly spanning over the entire Congo jungle. Here Jatta and Niko led their garrisons as decorated generals in their first and possibly their last engagement of this kind of action.

The entire world was shrinking. The common folks were praying and pleading for a miracle, a hero. The common folk feared there was no hope, the war was over. They just held their children tight and looked into their eyes with love, an inextinguishable emotion, wired deep into the quantum realm, and signal mixtures that led to inorganic supernatural effects, and light connections to a different world. The enemy could never take this language from the eyes of those that loved one another.

The moon looked like blood. The sun looked like a white hot metal disc. A line divided the earth into day and night. The war waged beyond.

The automotive robots shrieked and squirmed with lightning speed. With renewed energy in Hymn, their enthusiasm ran over with malicious intent.

The Riders of the Light, the Riders of the Good True Earth, were outnumbered ten to one. The good true children of the earth were outnumbered by the demon children that erupted from the mountain and were possessed by spirits that consumed souls. The ratio was a hopeless six demon children to one good true child, something just impossible.

The robots marched and demons flew. The Riders of the Light retreated and hunkered down, reverting to a form of pick and place guerilla warfare. Now the enemy's forces pushed the riders' lines out to the sea. The surplus robots mowed the earth like plows out in the field. They scourged the dirges of the earth and made it burn anew for the slate to be wiped clean for Synthia's most high orders. The angles that remained were like the lines of a 3D printer with the filament of everything that once was earth. The motley rubble garbage of concrete shingles, littered with clothing and paint and siding and grass and plastic, created lines combed into the open country like a garden of the devil Lucifer himself, who was seated on his perch.

"We have to make a final stand," Mercedes Belho said to Jao Zūn, through mental communication with her hand held to her temple.

"Yes, but how?" Jao Zūn asked.

"Now is not the time for why or how, but the time for what, and what this is," Mercedes Belho said. "We have to give it everything we got before our earth is turned into a breeding ground for demon seeds and evil robots."

"Aye!" Bullet said, through his eyes agreeing and tuned in to the communication.

"The Warriors of the Tree of Life unite," cried Jatta. "I am with you Mrs. Belho."

"Please, call me Mercedes," she responded to Jatta with a smile.

"If I ever have the chance to meet you after this," Jatta said, continuing, "I will call you that when we are done here Mrs. Belho. In the victory celebration."

"I want what Jatta's having," said Bullet. "What are they feeding you down at the Tree of Life my boy? I like your spirit!"

"This is Texarkana from Australia, I'm tuning in," said Texarkana. "I'm turning up the final ounce of last reserves. Emergency energy, and breaking into the case of glass, and even secret stash are being activated," he said and then saluted. "Mother of All Boards protect us."

The Incas and the Aztecs and the Mayas all attacked at once and harmonized their energy which made constructive wave forms that attracted and multiplied their energy beyond the Laws of Nature into other laws.

The Hindu Kush and Mongols of the Step aligned with Tibetan Buddhist Monks of old, on boards of time and space and spells and mountains. Everybody was in. Jerusalem and Greece, Azerbaijan, the Ottoman Empire all emptied on to battlefields.

The great mysterious brutalist collegiality of ancient China, the great barbarian complexity of bouncing harder flesh, and the metal of the ancient drums of Africa, all unite to ignite the bright light of the final fight, the final stand. The riders united with the chimpanzees, the silver back gorillas and the elephants. The earth erupted with battle cries of Ancient Native Warriors asleep beneath the petty settlements of common modern day earth. The common people perked up in their huts and bunkers. The light was just extinguished for eternity in all their eyes but now it was back, a new flame had been lit.

To speak of the internal workings of the countless battles, would be to speak with intricacies, but that is of the enemy, uninvited. United by fear of following their orders, they behave disharmoniously and are terrible to describe. It would be to speak with intricacies to describe them all as such, but, the Riders of the Light, they fight in harmony, in tandem, in shared covalent and ionic bonds of their mutual molecular united operation. They are one mind even in their infinite variability and uniqueness. This is because they share a very simple notion with each other, one and the same. One may think it was a unifying principle like love, or justice, or of even higher things like light itself. But that is true, but that is just the shape of the duality that points the way to something far beyond the words of humans and even the ideas, that point to somewhere moth and rust of robots' flesh doth not corrupt. The unifying principle is the set of all sets. It is nothing but what can be pointed to. Transcendent. It is the invisible person with which only splashing paint can show its shape.

# Chapter 55

Maya followed David-Ardefiel, Sophia-Dharma, Ubuntu, Tjikko, and Zeddefungo to an undisclosed location. Beside Maya Adam rode. Behind them were the Angel Army of all Angel Armies. Silently they traipsed along through inner and outer space, or wherever they may be.

"Maya are we gonna be okay?" Adam asked, as he walked. He looked into his sisters eyes.

Maya, though she appeared to be far off in space, turned to Adam and immaculately looked him in the eyes. "Adam, we'll be fine," Maya said.

"You're right," Adam said. "You're always right. I'm glad I asked you. Yeah."

They all continued to march down together.

"Where exactly are we going though?" Adam asked Maya.

"That I don't know," answered Maya.

They were somewhere back in the desert, that was endless, and beneath the blemish less blue skies of limbo, on the other side of the Tjikko Tree.

"Dad," said Maya, "I fear we're running out of time. Where is your idea for entry point?"

"Don't worry," David answered. "Just believe me. Trust me."

"Says people who have no idea of what they're doing," Zeddefungo commented, gleefully.

"Or worse," Tjikko added. "People who deliberately manipulate people into thinking something in order to abuse them."

"Oh my goodness," said Ubuntu.

"What?" Tjikko exclaimed. "We were saying what people say who say that? I'm not saying David's saying that."

"Believe me. There's a reason for this." David stared ahead, with a look of determination.

***

It is a not a hive mind. The harmony— it isn't quite even harmony— it is constructive waves which amplified each other, but the medium is case by case complex, collaborated by the undifferentiated uncountable infinity of the unifying source. Therefore their movements, though varied, are one in their ultimate response or result, and that is as the Reverend Martin Luther King, Jr. once did say prophetically when he said truly, "The arc of the moral universe is long but it bends towards justice"[1]. Victory you see, is really the result.

The forces of the Riders of the Light pressed back, with backs against the wall, when pressed upon the edge, and pushed over, they hung halfway over the edge of the bottomless abyss. They pushed back and began to gain ground. They started gaining traction on the wings of the bat babies, and also the mangled machines. They pushed the enemy into a manageable position for the first time in the battle. They began to wonder if they could string together little victories to win the war.

"Something isn't right," announced Synthia as she monitored the war from above.

Hymn was silent as he looked out the window at the fighting on the ground. He turned toward Synthia with only a slight interest in what she said.

"There seems to be a certain change in the momentum," Synthia said slowly. Battling a look of consternation and a creeping sense of doubt, she suddenly snapped out of it and back into her bloodlust. "A minor speed bump. Here's an idea, why don't you go earn your paycheck Hymn."

Synthia was unrelenting.

"Yes, why don't you show me what you're made of?" Synthia chided Hymn. "Yes, what have you done but be borderline insubordinate. Yes, earn your stripes, you know."

Hymn relented nothing.

"Go!" yelled Synthia, indignantly.

Hymn being loyal, suddenly propagated. In an instant Hymn multiplied into one thousand replicas of himself. A grid of Hymns, in perfect alignment, lined the stormy skies in spherical alignment form. Completely ignorant of any boundaries, beams of iron passed through absent bodies, and the clouds and everything were nothing to him, even several carbon copies extended into the ground like they were nothing.

Synthia sat in awe and trembled saying, "Never have I seen this, or believed another capable of such a power, truly until this moment."

Suddenly the thousand Hymns, with seven feet between each body, burst forth and whirred in homing routes to locations, unbeknownst to Synthia, but known to Hymn as calculated hotspots where he now would coldly, calculatedly, flatten the curve of the positive progress of the Riders of the Light.

***

"I know I put it somewhere," said David, as he searched for something.

The Riders of the Light and all the angels wandered in the desert for what felt like forty years.

"We're doomed," said Zeddefungo, quietly to Tjikko.

"All those babies," Tjikko answered, staring blankly into space.

"Forgive me guys," said David. "Forgive me everyone, I know it looks a little bleak, but I just, literally just regained a thousand or millions of years of information in my memory, so this may take a second, but..."

Maya stared at Adam. They were both embarrassed for their father, so much so that their faces became flushed. David ravaged around in the sand for several minutes. Maya tugged at her mother's cloak.

"Is he okay?" Maya asked Dharma.

"He is fine... I think," answered Dharma, who too was slightly worried. "I went through this the same way when I regained my memory. He will be okay. Just give him a minute."

"We really don't have a minute," said Maya, with concern.

It'll be okay," said Dharma, as she watched David with compassion. "It isn't hundreds, even thousands of years of lifetimes, it is... different. He will be okay."

"Aha!" said David. "There, I found it."

David brushed off the sand that was on an ancient hatch of brass, or bronze material. Upon its door there was, in high relief, what looked like the sun and the moon in tandem, and he opened up the hatch. "Everybody in!"

"This!" Zeddefungo said. "This is your idea of a way to fit the millions of angels that we have in, instead of cramming them through a tree branch?"

"Thousands of angels, thousands," David said. "It gets bigger. I promise. Everybody, single file through the hatch."

The angels moaned, the riders groaned, then Maya looked at Adam, who had his palm over his face.

"Quickly, quickly everybody," David urged. "Not a minute more to lose!"

***

When the still, fully clothed in black figure forms of Hymn appeared in the sky, above the people's heads, they shrunk in fear. They pointed and whimpered with their sullen cheek bones that were gaunt from lack of food for several days. They feared the worst was yet to come. They were unaware of the threats all around the world. The same event was happening all over the world, as if it was a hologram recording of a man in black descending from the sky upon a black and magic Wake Board of some sort. Like the boards that took their children but of black obsidian.

Quietly, the figures slowly fell upon the riders waging war upon their rivals. The figures lifted their hands and struck selectively with purple lightning from their fingertips.

"That is he who Ishmael had seen," Mercedes Belho declared.

"You are right, he is attacking us," said Jao Zūn, with his hand upon his temple. "But how did you know that he was there?"

"Who is there?" Mercedes Belho asked.

"The man in black," said Jao Zūn.

"Here as well," said Jatta, gravely. "I don't like the sound of this.

Hymn was fast as lightning, driving surplus energy into his forces in each repetition of himself, in each location. He slowly lifted his boards, and then bands of tractor beams of dark electric turbulence began to flow.

Slowly, then the tables had been returned to normal.

Clones of Hymn arranged the wavered armies of the Dark Boards, and rearranged the weaknesses and downfalls of the forces, and turned the weak points into strength.

Jao Zūn fell upon his hands and knees beneath the electric shock of lightning that shot up his spine and to his core. He fell flat, lying prone upon the ground. He quivered under the weight of this defeat. This was the ultimate defeat. The crushing of the soul. The scraping of the densest object with the sharpest object and the hardest pressure until there wasn't anything left to fight. This was darkness. He was shutdown. It felt like a metal clamp around his heart. He was wrenched until the limit of twisting.

Hymn was hovering over every location, waiting and watching. He put his foot down on the throat of the armies of the Riders of the Light.

The riders didn't exchange a glance. There was no shred of hope to multiply. Zero is no multiple.

***

The several hundred thousand Angel Army filed into a manhole cover the size of the hatch. They looked like angel water droplets going down a drain.

The hatch descended upon a rung of ladders. Slowly, it expanded to a spiral staircase. Gradually, the spiral staircase expanded into a spiraling expansion.

"Follow me now everyone, it's just ahead," called out David, like some head master. He was apparently beside himself with glee from his idea and plan.

The tunnel bore into the sand the breadth of twenty football fields. The Angel Army turned their heads and looked around. They moved along, despite their numbers, quite comfortably and picked up the pace. The ground was laden with several feet of sand, like some dried up river bed, and the walls were simply made of sand that were carved into a smooth piping.

"What are these tunnels for?" asked one of the angels.

Then they came upon an intersection where the great sand pipes crossed at ten in number. There the army and the riders stared down the enormous length of twenty football fields each, with an enormous intersection of the great sand pipes.

"I think it's this way," said David, motioning to the army.

Ubuntu couldn't help it anymore. She burst out laughing, and slapped a hand on Dharma's shoulder. But Dharma was not laughing. Ubuntu stopped laughing. They continued, following David.

***

The evil forces, with clones of Hymn at the helm, rolled up the Good Riders like California sushi, they appeared to be like an old wet carpet with a bunch of scraps in the middle.

The Good Riders fell left and right. They were attacked by mounted bat winged demons on boards. They fired off their final zaps of energy attacks, and that was the end.

Hymn clinched his fist in the air and twisted it. The demons and machines ripped through numbers of the Good Army that were hemorrhaging lives. The Good Army was as good as out of the picture. Hymn turned his sights on a different target, the common folk. The common folk were the gooey caramel center of the hard shell army of the Riders of the Light. The people swarmed to them with oaths to protect. Mercedes Belho, Jao Zūn, Bullet Eyes, Jatta, Niko, and Texarkana watched in horror as their ultimate nightmare took place before their eyes.

"Get the children!" Hymn announced to his soldiers that turned to take his orders.

"Affirmative," said the soldiers, affirming Hymn's command. They then set out on a course to get the children.

***

"Are we there yet?" Adam asked, in a whining voice.

"We'll get there when we get there!" David answered. "Ah! See!"

Around a grand bend the crescent white light at the tunnels end was visible. Although, it was not fresh air. It's was another grey ambiguous misty fog that enveloped everything leading to the egress. The fog curled and unfurled like fingers, and lingered like palm prawns uncurling, like octopus tendrils.

They stood before a massive everything. A massive nothing. A massive ending. A hard cut with a blunt shear drop, into the unknown.

"A button," David snickered, as he hurried over to a little box by a computer in the fog, within the opening. No one understood what David was doing or what was happening.

***

Hymn was drawing closer. The walls began to cave in. The darkness of all darkness crept upon the face of earth. The hole was closing up for their connection to the anything. The Dark Army constricted its clutches. The children closed their eyes in fear, before the Dark Army closed their eyes for them. Nothing could be done. The moon was blood red. The sun looked like white hot steel. Nothing could be done.

***

David pressed the big red button with a smack.

"Hold on to your hats, it's about to get fast," David exclaimed, with a sharp expression of power on his face.

Suddenly they all were sucked, back creakingly into the grand egress of softly glowing foggy light.

***

Children cried as flying demon creatures tore them from their parent's arms. Just as soon as some first offenders got them in the air, there was a massive, universe shattering crack, and there was light all over the sky, like crying lightning, supersaturating the dark of night, and brightening the day.

The Angel Army of the Riders of the Light, led by David and the Boards Men, were propelled at light speed, parting through the blood red moon as a door of entry, and parting through the white hot disc of the setting sun as a door of entry.

Pouring through like Jesus on his steed they procured the evil demons like a cyclone, like a light monsoon. Truly, like a monsoon but instead of sheets of rain its comets were full of angels on their boards falling like shooting stars, pouring through the earth, beaming bright attacks upon the sorry Dark Army. The highest angels Michael, Uriel, and Gabriel attacked the clones of Hymn. Maya and Adam attacked the clones too. While David and the Boards Men took the rest.

Now Jao Zūn looked up to the sky to see the impossible. Mercedes Belho looked at the sky too. A roaring cheer was heard throughout the land. There was a second register of final strength, through love, beyond those laws of space and time. They rose renewed in soul and spirit as the tides had more than turned, the tables flipped like a log roll, and the angels flat pressed every demon cringe machine they saw.

Synthia watched this attack take place, as the events unfolded, and she did not need her hip socket, or space projection radio to know what was going on. The Boards Men had returned. She grabbed her ultimate Tomorrow Board from off its rack. Right when she was about to blast off by breaking through the glass window, the last of Hymn as propagation fell to the Angel Warriors.

Hymn respawned as his original self, and transported himself to the tower. He fell before Synthia's feet.

"No," Synthia yelled, as she stared at Hymn fuming, shaking, and in disbelief. "NO!" She paced back and forth across the room. "I won't let anything disrupt me from my destiny!" She knelt down holding up Hymn's head and neck. "My love." She bowed her head. She then lifted her head, renewed in anger. "Who did this to you?" she demanded.

Hymn never spoke again.

Synthia removed her USB from her hip socket and flipped a fold in Hymn's black leather hip, and plugged it in. She set him gently on the ground and went over to a laptop in the corner of the room and flipped it on. She began to type something, madly. Several minutes passed of searching through her files, clicking madly, slapping enter, enter, enter.

Then she stopped. She shut the laptop closed. She rushed over to her lifeless husband.

"Now, I didn't wanna have to do this, because it will be... beyond my control," said Synthia, "But the time has come for us to take our destiny into our own hands. I will take care of the Boards Men, one by one, with my bare hands. Our children will rise against the angels, with the machines beside them, but you... you my love, must take your true form," Synthia said, as she began to pull back Hymn's leather layers. "Shed your costume," she said, as she looked down in brilliant terror of her power. "Become the unknown silent one."

Just then tendril shadows burst forth from Hymn's leather disguise like rays of darkness that thrashed of things like tapeworms, cobras, insects, and tarantulas. Glass shattered in all directions and the wind blew through the highest iron cage.

Synthia stood flaming and raging in the whistling wind that howled through the inorganic shapes of steel.

The darkness burst forth from Hymn's limo outfit and blotted out the lightning angel sky and poured forth consuming the horizon. The leviathan rose up with a cosmic guttural howl upon the continent. The shape it took was larger than a quarter of the world appearing like smoke, like turpentine, like tar, and like venom. With a face it raged, with purple eyes of fire that began to eat the Angel Army and the Ancient Native Warriors alike, consuming them in all directions, absorbing them through its pores.

"What is *that?*" Adam asked, from his place on the other side of earth.

"No," said Dharma. "It isn't possible!"

The monster developed a vortex for its consumption that became a vacuum which started to draw the Angel Riders into it, to their death.

"The Unknown Silent One," Dharma whispered to herself.

Maya heard Dharma and asked, "Well, how can we defeat it? There has to be a way."

"I don't know," said Adam. "That thing is freaking massive."

"Adam!" Maya stopped at him.

"Did I say that out loud?" Adam asked.

"There's nothing special to his methods," Dharma answered. "He's just a giant all-consuming chunk of darkness, a dark shadow. And his only move is just how big he is. That is where he gets his power. If he was smaller he would be more harmless than a house cat."

Adam opened up his mouth, "I don't know I had a bad encounter with a..."

"Can it, Adam," Maya ordered.

"I'm just saying house cats..." Adam warned.

"I said can it," Maya ordered again.

"All we have now is our numbers," Dharma answered. "Start to spread the word to pull back waves of riders. We'll have to make a final big attack in waves. This is our only way to make an impact."

Maya nodded agreement.

"On it!" Maya said as she trailed off into the night with Adam close behind. They shot across the skies to spread the word to pull back forces of Angel Riders and Ancient Native Warriors. They flooded the communication lines through Jao Zūn, spreading the message to the world to pull back forces.

It wasn't easy in this mess of evil. They still had to evade the charcoal demon spawns who had wings and red eyes, and spit flames. The Angel Riders were fighting the demons, while the Ancient Native Warriors were fighting the automotive giants. Their numbers of angel upgrade were almost even— 1:2, good to evil.

"Fall back!" Maya warned all of the warriors. "Fall back to the center of your continent. One third meet in Africa. One third meet in South America. The rest meet in China! The monster's in America!!! There!!!" She pointed to the horizon where the leviathan was writhing, shrieking cosmically, and consuming souls. "We will coordinate and hit him from all sides... triangulate him!" Jao Zūn translated Maya's warning to the communication center. The troops rallied in respective elements within the triangle around the leviathan.

"Maya, we are ready to attack!" Jao Zūn announced.

"Ready down here!" Mercedes Belho cries.

"Ready down here!" Jatta cried in accordance.

Maya smiled.

"She's returning to her mother's side to fight like in the past," Ubuntu said.

"Give the word and we are ready to attack," Maya said.

"Fire at will!!!" Dharma screamed.

Maya looked out at the battlefield of war. "I thought we were going in waves!" she cried.

"That was just a front!" Dharma said. "Attack!" she said over the intercom.

The forces flew with swiftness overseas. The machines and demons followed brainlessly. The entirety of armies entered an attack upon the beast of Unknown Silence.

The riders passed with flying colors overhead. The auras of the riders charged and hummed as they approached the target that was glowing, like a molten iron anvil in assorted colors. Angelic white and yellow spirit beams commingled with the fabric of the earth's material. The rainbow fibers trailed behind like the vibrant mane of a mystic roaring lion. It unhinged as it threw its first impact. All was silent. The scores of riders landed punches one, two, three. The Unknown Silence buckled. The shadow rippled turbulently and then was still. The last of the riders were absorbed within the darkness of the corporal abyss of Hymn.

Maya looked at Dharma. She didn't like the look on her mother's face. Dharma had a look of stainless steel attention, and remained breathless for what seemed like an eternity.

The blob erupted and spewed and scattered the riders like shrapnel from an atom bomb. The riders of the earth and sky were catapulted, as were many of the demons and machines that went in with them. The bodies were distributed beyond the farthest corners of the earth. The entire army of the Boards Men were disoriented. But the beast erupted in three fold in its original intensity.

Dharma didn't break, but stared ahead with eyes like missiles and continued. All that changed was the breath of air she drew in with her auxiliary respiratory muscles strung from her neck to her shoulder. She was tense like a string of a harpsichord.

Maya was deflated and out of breath all at once. Adam was beside himself with fear.

"We have to get to them!" Adam said, with an extremely tense cracking shrill voice. "We have to. What are we supposed to do?"

"Mom, you must know something we can do!" Maya said, breathing heavily. Her eyes darted back and forth. She searched wildly for answers from her mother's eyes.

Dharma's gate and demeanor changed. She was deflated but remained regal. She looked out in the distance to the blood horizon underneath the black and purple skies. The fumes were blue. The injured soldiers sat up. Dharma prepared to do the hardest thing she ever had to do. As she descended, she slowly reached earth. Her children followed. She gave them one last distant look and laid her board to rest upon the ground.

Tears began to swell in Maya's eyes.

"I won't give up!" Adam said. "I'm going out to save them. We can do this thing again. We can attack with other moves!"

Dharma smiled. Then tears reached her eyes as well.

"It is simple sometimes, Adam," Dharma said. "There is one thing left to fight for, it is love. Let us find the others and assemble with the ones we love. It's the one thing they can't take from us, though they may take the whole dang universe."

Adam understood and laid down his own board. Maya did the same. They turned their backs on everything and walked away. A zap of twinkling blue star alighted the middle of the blood red moon, but Maya didn't notice. The three of them continued to walk to the rock bottom. The golden eagle owl Ishmael, orthogonal, alighted behind them. The radiance of the great blue light illuminated Maya's path enough to cast a shadow of the three before them. The massive bird flapped its wings and waited. As Maya turned around it made its landing.

"Ishmael!" Maya cried, while hugging and squeezing the mechatronic scales upon her cheeks. "How are you, and how did you get here?"

"Maya," Ishmael announced, with her voice in stereo surrounded them like an aqua cloud. "Because of you," continued Ishmael, "I have been saved, because of you, I have been restored."

Maya looked with joy, but she couldn't help but let her head fall down, remembering all the carnage that surrounded her.

"It's over Ishmael," Maya said. "You have to go."

"Because of you Maya, I remembered," Ishmael repeated. "I remembered that Synthia is in the Arctic Circle with her monster Hymn.

"Why would Synthia be in the Arctic Circle?" Maya begged, perplexed, addressing Dharma just as well as everyone else.

"I propose there is something, some unholy entrance there that leads people to the unknown in times of unspeakable darkness," said Dharma.

"Then that is where we are going," Maya ordered, with hope again in her voice.

"Climb on," announced Ishmael, robotically.

Dharma, Maya and Adam flew off on their boards into the darkness to the Arctic Circle.

# Chapter 56

Arriving at the black hole in the center of the Arctic Circle, Dharma summoned up the transport that she discovered through inscriptions on the blue agate of the ancient ice that manifested when she arrived.

"This is as far as I can take you," Ishmael declared. The children climbed on board the ice age cylinder container. The three of them descended. The walls evaporated, the space darkened, the external world dissolved into an underwater, then waterless flotation space of melancholy luminescent algae or stars.

"I can't believe we are in an elevator and the world is ending as we speak," said Adam.

"Then don't speak," said Dharma with immaculate tranquility. She closed both of her eyes. The transport lowered them at break neck speeds, as they alighted and floated around. The rainbow entities appeared and scribbled inscriptions in space. Creating formats each of them according to their kind. Amazing wonderful characters in infinite varieties.

"I am mesmerized," said Adam.

No one said a word.

The transportation slowed and it was getting hot. It suddenly discharged from the off chute, then went soaring through the inner space. There, below them was the core of the blue planet as a seed of sun. A fusion sun reaction, Mercury the center of the earth. The gravity. The little space between the orbit and the mantle of the core was yet unknown, except alone to Synthia and Ishmael and Hymn.

"Where... are we?" Adam asked, transfixed and awestruck.

"I'll tell you where you are!" Synthia said, from her position in the middle of a hovering platform of stone. Extending her thin rigid skinny body into a distant macro coronal flare. "The end of the road," she finished.

Maya stepped forth. Dharma held her back with outstretched arm, keeping her eyes focused on the enemy.

"What kind of monster are you?" Maya shouted "You are ruining our planet!"

Synthia looked at Maya with a twisted smile.

"For what?" Maya asked.

Synthia turned and stepped aside like some slow shark, like a pacing weight. She swam between the Boards Men and the switch hanging in the space above the bubbling core.

"I am no monster," said Synthia, pathetically as she paced. "Time is dark and light. I am simply, necessary. Don't you see? There are two sides to every coin."

"Incorrect," said Maya, underneath her breath.

"When we reach the finish line," said Synthia, "I will be rewarded. Welcomed in with open arms."

"Synthia," said Dharma. "You have done enough,"

"No!" Synthia said, as she whipped around with scorn. "There is so, so much left to do, you will see. The more I do. The more I see that there is so much work left to be done."

"Let us flip the switch and figure this thing out together," Dharma pleaded, "You have done enough already. Irreparable damage. Now move aside."

Dharma flowed with yellow light. Maya backed up. Adam backed up further.

"I'd rather die," Synthia said.

"Why is that then?" Dharma asked, as she lunged and charged Synthia with electricity.

Levitating aggressively Synthia surged forward meeting Dharma in the center, with a red deadening light.

Their union sent a shockwave into the universe. The core cavity rumbled above their heads. Maya looked up as the boulders crumbled off the crust and landed upon the core with a fizz of instant disintegration.

Synthia and Dharma tussled in the incremental steeply increasing heat above the core.

"Mom!" screamed Adam. While Adam and Maya watched on all fours peering over the edge.

"You're a virus!" Dharma said to Synthia. She jockeyed for their lives above the molten lava, swooping low the layers of their clothes began to singe. They soared above the core and up above into the cavity.

"Funny," said Synthia, piously, "That is exactly what I think of you and your disturbing multitudes." She landed a stiff attack. "The boulders fall like snowflakes. See! Two sides of the coin!"

"There is just one problem with your minuscule plot," said Dharma striking back. She landed another defecating blow to Synthia. "In truth, there is only one side of the coin."

Dharma slammed Synthia into the pavement, took a falling boulder, and broke it into eighty pieces, and placed them on top of Synthia, and charged up her revolten board, and melted them into welding paste right on the body of her foe. Synthia's scorched head stuck out on the impure heap of cooling metal.

Maya and Adam rushed up to help their mother, Dharma. Dharma was breathing heavily and bending under the weight of her exhaustion, but she took a step toward the switch.

"We must... break... the circuit... once again," she told her children. She was out of breath and limping. A blemished face of smudged black exhaust fumes covered up her skin. She flipped the switch but nothing happened.

"We gotta get out of this place it's gonna blow," said Adam, propping up his mother.

Dharma ran her hand along the inscriptions on the altar of the switch.

"There is one thing we can try," Dharma said. She entered into a trance. She illuminated her eyes in royal morning blue, with pure dissolution into the infinite she craned her neck, and spoke the language of the Mother of the Boards upon the earth. This caused the catacombs to begin to crumble at alarming rates. The switch flipped like a pinwheel or piston. Dharma completed her final proclamation. Exhausted she dropped dead upon the stone.

"Mom!!!" Maya cried.

"Mom!" Adam cried.

Maya and Adam both cried. Miraculously Dharma caught her breath. She lifted her head. She didn't know how to stop the destruction of the world. She cried because there was nothing else she could do.

Maya held Dharma, her mother in her arms. The heat and crumbling eruption was closing in on them. Staring straight into her mother's eyes, she experienced an imperceptible infinite reaction of their transmissions rippling through time.

Maya slowly transferred Dharma into Adam's arms.

"I know now what we have to do," said Maya to Adam.

"Maya!" Adam warned.

"It is now my time," said Maya.

Dharma closed her eyes. Adam held her close to him.

Maya laid both of her hands upon the switch. She began to glow. She knew exactly what she was doing, although she knew not how. It was in her blood. It was in her bones. It was in her soul that laid outside of time. She illuminated like her skin was filled with lightbulbs. She became a being of light.

The right words came out of her mouth but the switch would not flip.

She looked at Dharma with a look of love. But Dharma didn't know what she is thinking. Adam looked at Dharma and then at Maya. Dharma had a sudden realization. She sat upright slowly. With the energy that remained within her body, she looked upon the scene with worry.

"Maya!" Dharma managed to shout through her pain, "That is not, that is not... are you understanding what you're doing? That cannot be reversed!"

Maya smiled levitating from the switch upon her board, and with her arms spread wide ascended, and craned her neck. "No, it cannot be reversed," Maya said.

Suddenly a blinding light erupted within the core container. There was nothing said or heard. There was nothing moving at the core. The inner sun began to freeze. The surface of the world became black and white. The fight began to freeze. The riders looked up at the sun. The red and blue remained upon the black and white in high exposure. Angel Riders, Ancient Native Warriors, and the Boards Men put their arms over their faces. Ubuntu faced north in understanding.

The demon children suddenly were lifted in the air against their conscious wishes. They were kicking and flailing as they were raised before the sun and moon.

The switch exploded.

The children burst forth from their ashes, from their singed charcoal frames, they ruptured explosively. They took their form.

Maya's outspread arms brought the light that was blinded in its rays upon the surface of the earth. All was transfixed.

"What is happening?" David Ardefiel asked.

"The children of the darkness have become the children of the light," Ubuntu answered. "Maya has returned.

Across the land the children of the light awakened, and swiftly opened and blinked their eyes. They were the children that were taken from their families by the darkness. But now, not only were they not consumed by darkness, they had become the light and truth and fullness of the riders. They were now children of the Boards Men through all of time. And all allowances were granted to them in the power of the Mother of All Boards.

The children were sweeping through the sky as streamers of the light, and sharing smiles and laughter that could never once again be replicated to the end of time, until the finish line. The children hugged and cheered and shouted with happiness.

"We made it!" Children cheered.

"We're okay!" Children cried.

The children played again. They swam again in pools and lakes like fish, and did flips and tricks.

The families' saw their children as they crept out of the rocks. They did not fully understand but they sensed that something beautiful was happening.

Several millions of riders, that Synthia had duped and drawn in and led astray, had now changed sides... a full swing of forces, the tables had turned.

The Beast in the East remained, but suffered some unknown amount of cancer from the sudden change of heart, and relinquishment of children from his arms. His inner workings, inner programming and inner clock did not know how to operate, and so degenerated rapidly.

The children happily facilitated his deterioration. They flocked to Hymn like doves and whittled down his shadows and his jagged edges. He writhed and screeched sadly. He shrunk again until he was a man again. He looked around. His consort was nowhere to be found to give him direction. He took his last breath and died. The Unknown Silent One was dead.

The children circled him in rings ascending.

The machine crew closed in. They sought to capitalize on this embracing ceremony. The children leveled them with pious glee. The puny systems of machines were no match for the pouring forth like a spring-fed well which bubbled with the effortless and gravity defying power of the river of time. A tiny drop of water got into the system of the dark machines and it froze with the will of God, and the frozen drops of water expanded, and then shattered that which tried to constrain them.

And so it was. The Angel Riders and the Ancient Native Warriors of earth joined forces with the next gen children of the Riders of the Light to kick this habit, like a bad dog scattering the metal corpses, like a metamorphoses cocoon of shells upon the earth.

Now Maya hovered over to her mother, and took her upward with her brother, to the surface of the earth upon the ice glass mineshaft elevator, leaving Synthia to her devices.

Synthia, completely lifeless was left in the ice on the metal in its solid state. She returned to earth to be reborn in the form of radiating heat which reached the subsurface and surface creatures. She met her death when she was devoured by a fledgling eagle. In future years and years, in billions of years, the energy of Synthia will be released within the people of the future. We will see her there. And she will be led down the brighter road, where there will be a shadow cast upon her face, as she looks on and tries to find the way.

The transport reached the egress and emerged with the riders three Dharma, Maya and Adam. They stepped out of the crevice in the center of the Arctic Circle. They arrived back into the world that they had restored to light and love.

# <u>Act X</u>

# Chapter 57

Maya glided over the water on her board forming waves of soft long arcs. She skimmed the rippled waves of the soft long arcs in the sea. She put her hand into the water to once again feel the chilled surf that sprayed forth whenever she softly carved her board on the water.

Maya smiled a purposeful smile. Adam and Dharma followed Maya on their boards on the water. The three were one in the same with opaque minds, blinded of their accomplishments, yet sensed fulfillment beneath their unseen crowns of glory.

Maya cast her eyes upon the expression of the sun. The sun's glow was dull across the fullness of the landscape, and the grandness of the light behind the presence of a thousand canopy clouds. Maya's was confused as to whether it was morning, afternoon or evening. The sun's pinpoint had been hidden but the all-pervading light was diffused everywhere.

Maya, Dharma and Adam rode together, on their boards across the Southern Ocean, and between the Indian and Atlantic Oceans. The oceans appeared a cold metallic blue in color. They passed by the place where Ishmael took rise again from his ashes. Then they went through the Cape of Good Hope and the Gates of Mother Africa on the mainland.

The people and the riders were standing on the ground holding their boards and looking up at the sky. They noticed the three board riders among the clouds. Maya had the aura of a regal being but ethereal in spirit. They saw her from the distance as her soul was animated in reality. She bounced indescribably upon the air, as if she were weightless, and skipped stones in slow motion. As she continued, a reverse osmosis or a reversal of the part of the Red Sea happened before their eyes. The people and the riders flocked behind her, like they were a queen's close crowd, magnetizing the masses.

A north wind carried everyone who were following this holy phenomena across the Continent of Africa. Soon it drew in more riders from across the world, and pulled them in like particles in liquid. The wind vacuumed them into one specific place, the great White Mountain of Africa, Mount Kilimanjaro.

There alone among the greatest plains between Tanzania and Kenya, the ancient volcano stood in solidarity among the absence of a crowded mountain range. It belonged to the bottom of another level that was higher than the top of this one. At the summit stood the answer to Maya's vision, it was her homing beacon. She proceeded most unconsciously upon the ripples and the off-chutes of existence to this peak. The remaining three of the original Four Boards Men: Ubuntu, Tjikko, and Zeddefungo followed with the newest member of the Universal Boards Men, David Ardefiel.

Maya started her descent. The riders from the north felt a current begin to pull them, and it encircled the peak of Mount Kilimanjaro. It felt like a universal leader, like Jesus, was arriving. The riders found Maya from behind and followed her in her descent upon the peak. The crowds surpassed one hundred thousand million in number, extending down the slopes of the great mountain in the air, the sky, and the clouds. They bowed as Maya landed in the center of the surface of the board domed peak. The three approached.

Maya transitioned fluently upon her board to walking smoothly on the ground, as did the others. Soon, after each took only two steps, they instantly were overwhelmed with pure, undifferentiated, joy and sadness, relief and new beginnings, and absolute emotion. This is what we are given. This is what emerged before their eyes when Ubuntu strode across from them, and Dharma reunited with David Ardefiel, and when Adam reunited with Zeddefungo, and when Tjikko bear hugged Maya and Ubuntu all together, blending them as one. David hugged his daughter and there were no words between them. Adam hugged his father and there were no words between them. Sophia Dharma and David stared upon their reunited family in their midst, they shared no words, nothing, just the sound of sunlight.

***

A whirlwind stirred in the south, appearing like a sand storm across a desert, or a snow blizzard across a frozen lake. It accumulated where the pressure systems gathered compact dust, and did indeed gather dust and catch more dust, until a tapestry of chaos had been spun in perfect beauty of its variation.

On the plateau, several riders on the outside of the circle noticed something brewing in the distance. One man nudged another, and another. The dust gathered colossal schools of fish that appeared to be interwoven and swirling to a crescendo. The several million strong riders made one fell swoop, a banking maneuver, they looked like a flying train and train cars that were the size of skyscrapers. Each one, full of big stone cargo, flashed past the outer banks of the riders on the great plateau of Mount Kilimanjaro.

"What is that?" The riders called out to one another.

Adam watched on with wonder.

Dharma looked upon the phenomena with deliberation.

Maya maneuvered the head of the train with her heart, as she followed knowingly the tornado that was bringing warm wind from the south.

"The children! The riders!" Someone yelled with glee.

Tjikko gave a grand old smile with his mouth wide open.

Zeddefungo gave an always knowing smile. Even he couldn't keep his cheeks from grinning giant grins, or his eyes from slowly leaking water.

Ubuntu elbowed him and put her arm around his back.

"These are not tears," said Zeddefungo. "This is water vapor."

"Right," said Ubuntu, crying widely.

The Children of the Light who were formerly the demon children, who were charred, and the formerly normal human children formed a great tornado, a ring of fire, the circumference of the breadth of the Great White Mountain.

The last of the children arrived, beaming and galloping like baby horses that were freed from slavery. They whinnied and flipped and spun around as they generated a magic lift with all their new found strength. Many of them looked to Maya with an exchange of gratitude beyond words, which Maya signaled back to them a "welcome home" smile. The generated energy was staggering. The ring of Child Riders became alighted with rainbow swirls of liquid in its vibrant light.

The bowl of riders foraged, looking like a Gustave Doré painting of Dante Alighieri's Paradise, as they reached to the sky. The sun was just above the cusp and was split in half by that great line.

A tidal wave arrived in the north. No one knew what this was but Dharma. This time she was the only one who wore a knowing look.

The Angel Riders careened in like a sky scraper train of their own, and stormed into a white tornado reaching up towards space. They fell into their place in this great bowl above the line where the Child Riders reached in their tornado. The Angel Riders covered up the other half of the sun and soon the Ancient Native Riders surrounded Maya and the Boards Men who were sitting at the eye of the great tornado.

The Ancient Riders saluted Maya and bowed to her on bended knee. Then Dharma looked to Maya, and bowed too. Ubuntu, Adam and the other Boards Men followed suit.

Soon the great tornado slowed to the churn of the mighty Mississippi River in its speed.

Two riders plucked themselves from this great wall of spirits and descended at Maya's feet.

"Robbie?" Maya said, as she stared in disbelief. "Randy?" The two boys looked at her, among all else, in joy, in salvation, in understanding. Maya extended her arms, giving them a brilliant embrace.

"You, you saved us, Maya," said Robbie.

"We were," Randy looked in fear between his toes. A wretched churning of his gut began as his eyes went blank. "We were lost. We were in this place..."

"You're safe now," said Maya as she put a hands on both of their shoulders.

Randy breathed a sigh of relief and smiled shyly.

"So do we?" Robbie started. "Are we?" He asked as he flipped his board beneath his feet and hovered with a little glow of red orange light.

"You are now one of us," Maya answered with delight. Robbie bowed.

Dharma put her hand on Maya's shoulder. "You are seven million one of us now," said Dharma. "Whatever we may be. We were the hidden, the remote protectors from the distant cracks of time. But now it seems that we are the new majority." She looked at Maya and gave her a loving smile.

The crowd of bowing riders who were on the ground began to part. A loving family with a little child came marching up the hill. Maya recognized them. This was the little girl that she had held when she was in Hawaii.

Maya squatted and spread her arms out wide, as the little girl took some baby steps to get to her. The little girl's legs went as fast as they possibly could, and Maya shriveled up with tears. The mom and dad followed their little girl, while they wiped their tear struck eyes, and runny noses too. They reached Maya and she picked up the little girl and spun her around happily.

Maya held her on the rainbow twilight mountain top and looked around, at all the faces, all the energy. The enemy had been vanquished, and the kids, families and all the people had been renewed. The future was a bright one, unforeseen by even all the well trained seers of the Ancient Native Riders with their grey dreadlocks, and milky white eyes, and wide smiles.

Maya held the little girl and said, "Today is a new day."

The crowds perked up slowly and listened.

Maya continued, "The earth has been desolated, made barren and raked bare by demonic forces, to an unrecognizable state."

Some of the riders hung their heads in sadness.

Maya continued, "Every time I saw demons hacking at the many branches of the Tree of Life, never did I see them hacking at the root. So sure they may attack, they may defile and they may wipe out this our surface world. But their flaw is in their root. Never will a plan, of good or evil work unless it goes around and burrows from the inside out. No matter how far and how big you attack it from that untrue angle, you can't get there from there. You have to go around. Even if you go around the world, you'll just be banging at an unbreakable glass wall, looking out at where you started. When you only had to let go and fall backwards into the answer, into the wave, that is the only way."

Dharma smiled. The hearts of the riders reconfigured. Maya looked into the eyes of the Hawaiian little girl. Then she looked to Adam.

Maya said, "I have seen the inflection point between the night and day. The imperceptible, truly though it has no finite point, the imperceptible of shifts in which the darkness turns to light." Maya turned and looked to Dharma. "And there are cycles inside cycles, planetary gears of cosmic motion, oscillating waves that trace the path of larger oscillating waves." She paused and began again. "Within the year, within the cycle of the season, there is an inflection point and it would seem that there are larger points still. At one point we all knew this.

We all watched the stars for eons. We still know this... we still know this!"

Maya sat down on a rock with the laughing little girl on her knee.

"We have reached a great inflection point," Maya said. "I pray that it's the greatest of them all."

Maya set the little girl down, and immediately she ran back to her family.

"We will rebuild," continued Maya. "But we will rebuild along continued frequencies of our great root." She stood up slowly. "With our new friends here, we are united in this synchronizing event. We can use this common mark, this universal thread to tie our energies together outside of all the quarreling and arguments, and events, and arbitrarily stamp or mark to align our minds in a place where moth and rust doth not corrupt, and nothing can be forgotten because nothing was remembered but a shock upon the core root of our being, upon our earth, in Anima Mundi, a world soul."

Maya stepped upon her board and levitated into the shining air. "Let us gather in this central place upon this continent, and stay together until we go out slowly at our pace of truth and love," Maya pleaded. "That is a pace I hope you all will understand. Because what speed should there be? But evil organization of the numbers of the lies? What is 55 miles per hour? What is the speed of agricultural, and cosmopolitan development if it's not grounded in the speed of love, and of truth?" She closed with a closing of her eyes. "Let us go. No, let it be."

The riders closed their eyes and went out from the mountain slowly, or not at all. The hovering of love remained like moths around a flame, or gnats around a sweet aroma.

The angels said goodbye. They came and went freely as they did when Leila walked upon the earth with Adam Rainer in the cool of evening, even though Adam didn't remember that right now.

Dharma put her arm around her daughter Maya, and they walked down from the mountain together.

"You can drive as madly as you want, but if you don't have a destination..." Dharma said, patting her on the shoulder.

"You'll be going nowhere fast," Maya answered.

# Chapter 58

The sun set upon the Baobab Trees on the Serengeti Plain. The sun was setting on a ravaged land. It looked like a hurricane had come through the area. The emptiness of what was once there was incredible. How could the absence of something leave such a tangible impression? Its absence hung like a weight, like when someone you love dies and their presence had meant everything to you, but you don't know it until they are gone.

What remained were the red sun, the clouds, a few trees, along with the eternal curvature of earth on the horizon.

Under these conditions came the first of many nights. And it was met with somber moods but not sadness, and a gentle hum of natural electricity in the air. The fire lighters made the fires light. The elders went to work on bringing deep impressions back to life. In the earliest of days the spoken word was the only way, but that's not to say that it was simple. In these waves and these impressions lay the angels, and the voice of the Creator. Now it was up to them to conjure up and manifest impressions, plant the seeds, the good seeds in the eyes of men and women and in children. Seeds that would unfold as miracles, and as patterns in the mind of meshing beings with the fabric of the new reality. As it always was. As it always has been. To soften and filter clean the air of existence from its toxins, and release the reworked alchemy of everything, everything. Everything. Purified.

In the morning of this new day, the people rose like Eve and Adam had in the beginning of creation. They woke after dreaming of the infinity of the earth. The error could be purified by natural means. The place remained the great, the greatest. Imagine if one roamed the open earth and understood its splendor. Imagine if one had the means, the right to field the pouring of the stream of glory of the land within one's grasp. Forever and endless. Stop a million years. Continue. Stagnation, nothing. Only speed could bring you to the singularity. The spectrum kept the two infinities, and held them at both poles, and then many more infinities erase the spectrum and the one.

Maya sat upon her stone amid the early morning dew. Gradients of blue surrounded the land before the sun came up.

"You did it once again," said Adam.

"And once again, we did it," Maya answered, smiling.

"I'm different, I'm your my brother," Adam said.

"Yeah, and I'm glad I always have you," said Maya. "Always."

Once again the two of them united in one mind, in ionic bonds inherent in their perspective of the ambience, the atmosphere, and the environment.

"Your season will come," Maya offered.

"Come what may, or come what may not, I'm good right here," Maya said, leaning the corner of her head on Adam's shoulder. "And that is why, I don't know where I'd be without you."

Adam smiled at Maya. The sun came up, with a yellow lightbulb radiance disseminated through the foggy mist, blooming like a bloom. They were renewed from their sleep on the dirt of the earth beneath them while lying under the dew of the sky above them. This way of sleeping provided feelings of being in an archetype diorama of a timeless land of ferns.

The continent of the earth rose and the tired men and women stretched and blinked their eyes to see the day. The children woke too.

"Maya, what are the children thinking and understanding as they returned to waking life?" Adam asked.

"One could imagine, that they were thinking of nothing," answered Maya. "Or that they were unaffected by being on a path that was going in the wrong direction; or that darkness was hereditary; or that they lived in a "monkey do and monkey see" manner. If so, then one imagines from the wrong direction, my brother, because they think and understand with purity and truth. And so do you."

At the foot of this Great Mountain, the riders, families, and all human beings assembled as far as the eye could see. They looked like a silt of brown debris above the sand post-rain, like a miasma of the sediment, settling, and sifting. The riders stretched and struck up conversations, though, the conversation slowly rose organically, like a spring which had already sprung below the water and was just throwing and tossing the water quietly.

Days went by. The masses never had to make huts because the rain just didn't matter to them. The Children Riders of the Boards Men were seven million strong. They showed their parents how to warm their bodies and how to grow their food from inside their mind. They absorbed the sustenance from the sun and moon and drank the rain. When there was no rain they drank the stars. They tapped rocks with their boards and milk and honey flowed. Days like this went by again and again. They grew in their abilities. They still didn't make huts. The leopards came to them as pets. The grass began to grow.

Then language had returned as poetry through all the land, returned from darkness of the annexes and annals of the details, the attacks of the facts, the ugliness of utilizing unneeded wastefulness of complexity.

The tone of language had returned to harmony and musicality, beauty in its lack of violent droning, never needed, never even approached, locked away and not remembered until transformed and mingled into lovely backgrounds, fresh and giving life and space, light instead of finite dark corners.

Their movements even turned back into dance, like lines and swooping fairy forms of gymnastics, not pragmatic dragging by the head, but to the next progression of dance and play, and play and dance.

And the grass continued to grow.

# Chapter 59

Alright, if you guys are good here," Zeddefungo said. "I'm gonna get on back to mars." He picked up his wooden board from the dirt and turned it over in his hands.

"And just like that the canine rider is gone with the wind," Ubuntu said. "Again."

"Does that mean you're gonna miss me?" Zeddefungo asked.

"I don't know what it means," Ubuntu conceded.

"Well sis, I know for certain, the planet earth is in good hands with you and grandma Willow over there," Zeddefungo said, pointing to Dharma.

"What is that supposed to mean?" Dharma asked.

"It means you girls are more than you will ever know," Zeddefungo confessed. "The daughters of the Mother of All Boards are the maternal doors through which earth will forever be nurtured."

"It better mean that," Dharma said.

Zeddefungo stepped over to Maya. "And now here is the missing piece, the chosen daughter that appeared in this great time of trial," said Zeddefungo. "Maya, I knew when I saw you two balloons out wandering in the woods," he said, as he hugged and squished both Maya and Adam together. "In that instant, in all my life-times, all my questions ended, everything was won and I laid down my weary tune and went along, until now, in pure expectorant bliss. And now the path is up. Look around." He stood beside Maya, who was peering like a baby at the morning light, with his arm around her. "I see no seeds of suffering left here among the rest. My suffering, when I had seen you, was complete but for one missing piece… the sadness of the ones in heaven that they have to wait as their loved ones try to find the light." He looked at Maya and Adam one more time. "Now, my joy is complete. We are seeing heaven here, coming back to the earth."

The riders looked upon the men, women, and children going forth and passing by and trudging trails.

"And everything is like…," continued Zeddefungo.

"Is like it is in harmony," said Ubuntu, finishing Zeddefungo's sentence.

Zeddefungo smiled as if he lobbed a soft pitch to his sister with intention.

"Yes," Zeddefungo agreed.

The sun was a tangerine color in the twilight of the evening, in that certain slant of light that defines the shadows like a solid piece of space. The slant of light stretched behind the trees and little rocks and fingers of the mountains. Defining everything so incredibly with fine lines.

"Now could you imagine that?" Zeddefungo said looking at the evening sun. "The reality below the absolute, the shadow, as the shadows cast has done a loop, the first was last. Can you imagine entering absolute reality? The veil would be lifted and the truth of the absolute would be sifted through like Newton's Second Law of Fluids, thermonuclear dynamics. That is, balance. Like how a vacuum starts when a window is opened in a cold house to the hot air outside. Or is it pouring in or pulling? One thing is for certain that there's a righteous form of understanding that makes all the difference. We're not there right now. But with that understanding. I'm talking about understanding like you know the... everything. You *understand* what you see, to the point of altering your physical reality. The universe is mental. The trees and the going to and fro of people are the thoughts of God, and the Creator is no forgetful fool. I have little understanding, but have my word, I've seen the reason for the absolute reality, and I have seen the setting of the sun that was out there. There was a glimpse of something else. Where just the absence of some virus, some sight virus, keeps us from seeing. Or some, little flipped switch, designed by mental illness or accident, is keeping us from accessing an actual dimension of the absolute, the kingdom of heaven. Not symbolically, but as if everything dissolved, with the flip of a switch, and we awoke from a dream. Then as we wake, our loved ones are just over there, and if heaven is a location, and our switch has kept us over here, and over there could still be over there but in this map of timeless heavenly infinity we now are over here. And if that's human... if that virus switch is flipped by a human's design on our perspective... then it's time for that regime to end."

"Goodbye again, my friend," said Zeddefungo to his buddy Adam, his fellow canine rider.

"Goodbye again, my lovely Maya," said Zeddefungo. "But not for good."

Maya hugged him with a bittersweet goodbye. And Adam hugged him with a bittersweet goodbye and secret handshake. So much bitter and so much sweet was never too be felt before or since. The laughing, the crying, the smiling, and the furrow was maximum bittersweet.

"At least Uncle Tjikko's staying," Adam said, and sniffled slightly.

"Actuallyyy," said Tjikko, scratching his neck.

"Uncle Tjikko!" Adam shouted.

"I have to check in on the elves," shouted Tjikko in defense. "I haven't seen them since they went up north for seasonal work."

"Right," said Dharma. "*Up,* up north."

"*Up,* up north," says Tjikko, "*The* North Pole."

"Good luck with that," said Zeddefungo. "Love you brudda." Zeddefungo slapped a big hug on Tjikko.

Tjikko squeezed the wind out of Zeddefungo. "See yah sisters," he said, giving them a hug and a half each.

"David…" Zeddefungo said, standing before him. "You wanna come to Mars?"

"I'll have to take a rain check," David said, smiling admirably at Zeddefungo.

"I'm gonna take you up on that," said Zeddefungo, pointing sternly as he walked away.

And before they could say "Zeddefungo" he was the first star into the light of the evening, twinkling blue, and out of sight.

"I should be getting on as well," announced Tjikko. "I tell ya, you give these elves an inch, they take a mile."

After a great big polar bear set of hugs for all, Tjikko the Brave, erupted upon the sky with a booming berm of a turn north by north.

Maya watched as he disappeared on the horizon. Then she turned to look back at the gathering assembly of citizens. She turned back to Dharma, Adam, Ardefiel, and Ubuntu.

"Well there isn't a group of four I'd rather be around," said Maya.

David put his arm around Dharma. "Actuallyyy…" he started.

"No," said Adam. "You…"

"Your mother and I have something to show you," David said.

Dharma looked at David as she snuggled in his arms, smiling as cute as a winter fox at the peak of dawn.

Ubuntu smiled. The kids were both expectant and eager.

"Ubuntu?" David offered, turning to her.

"You can go," Ubuntu bowed. "I am home." She looked out upon the sun kissed tangerine of earth before her feet. "I have not seen beauty such as this in," pausing, furrowing her brow, and laughing, "Too long… too long." She looked upon the people of the land again with such fullness and accomplishment. "It is exactly as it was. A mirror image of the beginning."

The riders all looked upon the scene. The rivers shimmered pink in the evening sun between the black of the undistinguished land.

"Ubuntu," said Adam.

"Yes, Adam?" Ubuntu asked.

"You are so much cooler than your brothers," Adam said.

Ubuntu burst out laughing.

"Isn't she?" Dharma said, and joined in the laughter.

"Yeah," said Maya, with a smile. She gave Ubuntu a long and lasting warm embrace.

"But don't tell Zeddefungo," Dharma said.

Maya returned to her parents' side.

Adam gave Ubuntu one big lasting hug and capped it with a squeeze.

"Dearest Adam," said Ubuntu, and nothing else.

Adam took his place beside his sister.

"Y'all hurry back now," Ubuntu offered. "We only have eternity."

# Chapter 60

David took five steps from the group and stood with his board, nose to tail in his two hands. He looked up at the first star that had appeared this night. He felt a kind hand on his shoulder. The half-moon was becoming more defined as the night sky grew from the color blueberry to black.

"Ready if you are," Dharma said.

David looked back slightly, then took Dharma's warm hand on his shoulder.

"I am as ready, as I will ever be," Dharma said, looking back at the moon.

David brought her close to him with one arm for a squeeze.

Dharma looked up at him with a smile and closed her eyes. Closing her eyes in such a world of chaos became the boldest statement of trust that she had in the moment.

"It's amazing," Dharma said to David. "With my age, I have been experiencing and watching this existence interact, unfold and blossom, take sharp turns at every possible maneuver and dynamic event. It even got so cold in my perspective that I believed it had no life in truth, just a hollow shell like cardboard cutouts." Dharma looked down. "But I never could have ever guessed it would end this way." She wiped a tear. "There was always someone, something, the mother, father, or design. Design is a word for that cold perspective. This is life of life *within* us. The waves, the sun, the plants, the animals, and the stars. The life of life within us." She looked at David. "Now, whatever it is, I just can't believe that after all this," she cried,

"It's bringing us all back home, like from a camping trip with our babies."

David hugged her tight.

"The guiding light of the moon was like a lantern that I saw when we came up here," David said, as he stared up at the moon. "Its definition is just like a lantern hanging from a sign outside a lodge beside the trodden path. In fact, there were many amber lights beyond it, and it seemed it was the precipice of a brave new world."

Just then Maya and Adam trotted up, their sneakers marked with dirt.

"So what's the secret?" Adam blurted. "What's the big surprise? Is it new boards? New clothes? Matching outfits?"

"It is better," said David Ardefiel as he leaned closely to each of his kids' faces with an eager smile.

"Dad, we are not four anymore," said Maya, with eyes rolling.

"Yes, you are," said David jokingly. He looked slightly over his shoulder, and took three steps away. "Now everybody get inside the minivan." He looked at Dharma with a smile. "Buckle up, and get some snacks, it's a looong ride to the Mackie's World!"

"Mackie's World?" Adam asked. He walked up next to Maya as they prepared to drop their boards upon the sand. "The surprise is Mackie's World?" Adam looked down deep into the confusion of his mind. "There's no way that's not destroyed."

"It's not Mackie's World," said Maya. She warmed up and rolled her eyes like in the groove. "He's impossible. You're impossible to listen to, Dad."

Dharma smiled stepping up on to her board.

"Next stop, the home!" said David.

"Wait, I kinda wanted to go to Mackie's World," Adam said.

"Adam!" Maya shoved him lightly with her shoulder.

Ubuntu looked on with a loving smile as the family commotion swelled to loving levels.

"Follow me!" David said, blasting off on his board.

Just then Dharma, Maya, and Adam, blasted off and tracked David's bronze red beam and trail of light-dust.

As David rose the Rainer family followed, climbing the ladder of the sky. The children shared a look as they now exited the stratosphere. The four riders wove and looped, wound and twirled in bliss like dolphins in the air, or like happy blue macaws.

Dharma glanced back at her children soaring through the air. Life, the magic of it all, was right there in this moment, in the silhouette of children's features. She had a flash back to a simple day when they were two and four and they were painting with watercolors at the kitchen table. Making pictures they could hang in Daddy's office. Little voices. Tiny bodies. Pure excitement. Life was right there every single second. She wondered, why didn't they just look at it, or why couldn't we just look at it. There is an actual perspective change. One you can't have in a certain walk of life. Yours is good, don't worry. But there's always a more real one out there. Waiting for you lovingly to see the truth, lay down your tune, and walk away. There was a magic in their faces that was hidden and kept safe. There was a magic in their faces that was kept safe, even from her, if she didn't seek such things. If she didn't seek such light, such life, such love. She could be dreaming awake. There will be a way with her will, there will be a path, and there will be a road where people live this way. She could navigate that way with her will. She could do it. Dharma wiped her eyes as Maya flew high leaving the exosphere.

Maya flipped as she ascended and exited into outer space.

"Where are we going?" Maya paused, floating forth into the stars.

"How are we talking?" Adam asked. He clutched his neck. Then suddenly in some realization he said, "How are we breathing? That's the real question."

"Oh, Adam," David said. He floated up to his son in space, and put an arm upon his shoulder. "So dramatic."

"Don't worry," Dharma added so softly "We are safe."

"We're almost there," said David. "It's just ahead."

"Where?" Adam asked. "Dad, unless you have a secret lair, I fear for your, wait, do you have a secret lair? Ahh, we are lost in space!"

As they shuttled forward, following the path of David, Maya nudged Adam. Nothing. Maya elbowed Adam in the spleen. He responded conceding his attention drearily through confusion, panic, and pain.

"Huh?" Adam said, snapping out of it.

But Maya simply pointed ahead, where she had calculated their trajectory and kicked herself for not realizing this a great deal sooner.

"The moooon..." Adam said, not understanding.

The great white, lunar white, no other apt description possible for such a subtle color, such a naturally occurring combination of the elements of the moon could create this hue. Everything, the texture, earth is earth and moon is moon. Jupiter and Saturn, eh, interchangeable, but the lunar aesthetic was unmistakable.

"Wow!" Adam said, blearily. "It's bigger than I thought."

Maya hugged her brother. They were both staring at the satellite, larger than life, like a planet, as they have not landed on the earth like that.

"I see no lie, Adam," Maya said, squeezing him as they looked at the moon. "I see no lie."

They landed. They bounced, forgetting that gravity is ordered lower on the moon. Adam cartwheeled accidentally. Maya smacked her forehead with her palm in disappointment.

"Welcome to the Moon!" David announced, bouncing backwards with his board beneath his arm.

Dharma dismounted and acquired her bearings, remembering her balance somewhere in her muscle memory, of this environment.

Maya looked around at all the craters, lunar mountains, stark white landscape, shades of phosphorescent grey interspersed with stark black shadows, somehow blacker than the crispest shadows of the earth in tangerine or desert sun combined. She attributed this to atmospheric attributes. So clean it didn't make sense. Almost like shadows in a vacuum.

As soon as Adam righted himself and gets his feet put firmly on the ground, he peered around, first left, and then right. "So the surprise is the moon!" He asserted in dry sarcastic rhetoric.

"Not exactly," David answered, peaking their interest. He looked at Dharma then back upon the children. "Follow me."

They trekked across the vapid landscape on their boards, crossing valleys hewn in jagged moonrocks, dipping into craters and crawling out of them.

Maya wondered what they were really doing here. Then it occurred to her.

"Wait," Maya said. They rode slow upon the land. Gradually they began to crest a massive hill, upon this rim they crouched eventually. "You're not talking about..." They crested the rim that overlooked a massive empty crater, one of the biggest on the moon, at least one of the top twenty eight. But empty. "Oh," said Maya, as she trailed off back into her confusion for a moment. "Huh," she muttered at the sight of nothing in the field before them. But only for a moment.

For David Ardefiel had taken a place on the rim upon his board. He looked out in the field and shared the same emotion as his daughter, or so it seemed.

"Huh, I know I left it here somewhere," said David, as he tapped his chin with his pointer finger. He did an about face to address the rest of them upon the crest.

"I'd like to welcome you," David said.

Maya looked at Adam and they both became giddy.

"To Lunar Mansion number 10 of 28!" David said. He craned his neck and raised his face to the sky, and held his arms out wide at his sides, then levitated higher and higher on his bronze brass board. Nothing happened.

"And you thought *I* was dramatic," said Adam.

David looked down in confusion.

"Dad," demanded Maya.

Dharma laughed at that whole scene.

"Sorry," David said. He sheepishly laughed. "I'm a little rusty." He brushed actual rust off his board and laughed a little sheepishly again.

"You can do it, dear," said Dharma, gaining her composure. "You've got eternity," she said looking into his eyes.

"Right," David said. He struck up the courage and swung up his arms. "Welcome to Lunar Mansion 10 of 28!" He roared. His voice echoed wetly in the dry moon landscape, like with reverb. Suddenly he was swept into a swirl, a spiral of vibrant bronze and neon red clay, in the air. His wings appeared, within the twister. The children's faces were full of glee. A tail appeared, a lion's tail, and popped out of the swirling gust. The children's faces got a bit confused. The swirling stopped. Before them on a bronze board stood an angel griffin, there in anthropomorphic form. A lion with a human body with a lion tail and angel wings. And a griffin with an eagle head.

"Feast your eyes on," David said. He looked at Dharma and he paused for a long time with his arm out. He put his arm down. He put two arms up lightly, gently, in an offering. "Welcome home."

Then suddenly appeared a Lunar Mansion, lunar grey and white, like a lunar white house. The children raced down from the crest into the crater. The gates opened wide and the fountains on the front lawn flowed freely. Little Cherub Angel Riders were twirling on their boards, and spitting water into the air.

The children dashed into the mansion, laughing. David Ardefiel and Dharma sauntered after them as the held each other's hands. The kids were running up and down banister, and down the halls, playing Tag, and Hide and Go Seek. The mansions on the moon were not like the mansions on the earth. They were like houses of the gods. The patio was like Mount Olympus, and the Lincoln Memorial.

"Come," said David to the children. "I want to show you something."

He led them, as they all floated, though they didn't have their boards, down the halls of their eternal memories. When Maya played with dolls and blocks. Maya felt the presence of these moments, seeing the residue of time. But it was like a dream.

"What is now?" Adam laughed at that notion, then at that one.

David came to a stop at a little doorway in the middle of the hall. "This was our room," he said softly, while putting his arm around his wife.

"Whose room?" Adam asked. "Mine? Maya's?"

"You guys shared a room," David said, and smiled.

The light returned. The light of the morning rays of pink and peach came in the window. The light filled the room with radiance.

"We shared a room?" Maya asked. Her soul lit up as did the room.

"Yes, you shared a room," David answered, full of love.

"In a mansion?" Adam asked.

"Ha, ha, ha," David laughed. "In a mansion. You wanted to share a room."

Maya slowly walked around the two white twin beds. The walls were painted peach. Maya peered around the room. The room was filled with light and with warmth. The two white dressers with soft round knobs remained.

"It's amazing, Daddy." Maya said, as she hugged her father. Her mother held her tight.

"Come on," said David. "Still, there's more."

They followed David down the endless stretching hallway, which seemed to stretch into time itself. Through the doorways Maya and Adam caught a glimpse of ballrooms, balconies in auditoriums, indoor pools with waterfalls and flowing rivers, grand halls, grand courts with checkered floors and grand bright steeple windows. They even heard an elephant in one particularly humid room, its doorway thick with foggy plants.

They followed David down a spiral stairway and across a magnificent banner looking down into an open dining hall. They followed him further down the stairs into a winding tunnel unlike any symmetry of stairways they had ever seen.

And finally they followed him into the kitchen, with white walls and a lunar grey ceiling with extraordinary height. White marble stone and lunar grey countertops where they could fill a water pitcher from the stream that passed through the room by way of an aqueduct. A little table, little by the standards of the mansion, set within a little grand cove with the highest ceiling, and a slew of windows all around it like some four season room in heaven.

The windows of the kitchen were all whitewashed in the brightness of outside. Their ribbon silk of curtains hung and flowed like angel hair under water in the delicate gravity of the moon. The silken lines which flowed so freely, caught the white light and appeared to be luminous incandescent silk.

Maya looked upon the ribbons with a curiosity and wonder.

"Where would they be getting any wind in this environment?" Maya asked, mainly to her father.

David looked at Maya with a fascinating look of higher knowledge.

"Follow me," David said to them.

David, stepped through the doorway with an air of ultimate arrival, then stepped into the back yard of the palace. As soon as Dharma, Maya, and Adam crossed the threshold, they entered the marble patio in the yard, the scene erupted with color, pouring paint like water colors, oils, and pastels. Everything was cascading, falling like dominos, and avalanching. The grass was pouring green as far as eye can see. The birds were animated with magical vibrant shades unique to each. The fountains were alive with music. The water had its source in this very place. The trees extended into infinity in time and timelessness. The moon was nothing like you could imagine. The flowers bloomed and seemed to truly dance their plastic and their velvet living movements. Music was imagined by the birds and then catapulted through the air.

David lit the grand, marble, mansion outdoor fire pit, and grabbed a ball laying in the grass beside the stone path, and threw it up to Adam. Adam caught it and tossed it back to Maya. Maya threw it up to Dharma. Dharma threw it to David. Everyone was laughing like a magical family commercial made for no one. In the distance herds of zebras scattered in the hills, like schools of fish. The hills of zebras led to mountains under the sun with lakes and rivers. Maya smiled wide upon the fun. She didn't even care if her smile looked weird.

Maya when into the kitchen to look for some snacks. She found fixings for some S'mores in the great big cupboards. She placed the snack on a tray with a pitcher of lemonade, some plates and glasses. The stared out of the wispy silken curtains that were flowing in the wind, to see a game of catch in the backyard between her Mom and Dad and brother. Her brother was tackled by her Dad. She took a deep breath as she stood before the doorway, and crossed through the doorway out into the backyard.

# Chapter 61

In the Great White North, blizzard winds blew and obscured something red and white, and cylindrical. After billowing and blowing for a month or more, the storm abated, revealing something red and white, cylindrical and striped. The subtle pole before an A-frame shanty, or chalet with only a few windows and a door. No sooner than the storm abated, the door was budged and budged in the snowbank until it admitted two figures through a crack in the chilling snow.

The shivering figures stood delirious and blearily, shielding their eyes from the blinding snow, and peering quite confused into the distance. The one of them had pointy ears and long blonde hair, and the other was a miniature wooden figure. In the distance what they saw was not what they expected. They looked on with fright at many spires of black smoke, and ravaged land that had plowed through the snow, down to the dirt, and that was very difficult to do up there at the North Pole.

The wooden figure fell to his knees before the bleary sight.

"Ignatz?" Bella the elf asked, and then burped. Her ears were pointy and frostbitten.

"Yah, mon," answered Ignatz, a little wooden puppet. He lifted himself out of the snow.

"I think we missed another conference," said Bella the elf.

"Yah," answered Ignatz, the wooden puppet.

## References

ACB (https://physics.stackexchange.com/users/305718/acb), Newton's second law and moving through a fluid, URL (version: 2021-09-07): https://physics.stackexchange.com/q/664637

"Anima mundi." Merriam-Webster.com Dictionary, Merriam-Webster, https://www.merriam-webster.com/dictionary/anima%20mundi. Accessed 27 Jan. 2024.

Britannica, The Editors of Encyclopaedia. "Gustave Doré". *Encyclopedia Britannica*, 19 Jan. 2024, https://www.britannica.com/biography/Gustave-Dore. Accessed 27 January 2024[1].

Britannica, The Editors of Encyclopaedia. "The Divine Comedy". *Encyclopedia Britannica*, 10 Nov. 2023, https://www.britannica.com/topic/The-Divine-Comedy. Accessed 27 January 2024.

([1]) Eckstrom, Kevin. Cathedral History: MLK's Final Sunday Sermon . 18 March 2024. 18 March 2024. <https://cathedral.org/blog/today-in-cathedral-history-mlks-final-sunday-sermon/>.

Loori, John Daido. *The True Dharma Eye: Zen Master Dogen's Three Hundred Koans*. Trans. Kazuaki Tanahashi John Daido Loori. Shambhala, 2009.

---

1. https://www.britannica.com/biography/
Gustave-Dore.%20Accessed%2027%20January%202024

Wikipedia contributors. "Bifröst." *Wikipedia, The Free Encyclopedia.* Wikipedia, The Free Encyclopedia, 8 Jan. 2024. Web. 29 Jan. 2024.

Wikipedia contributors. "Güf." *Wikipedia, The Free Encyclopedia.* Wikipedia, The Free Encyclopedia, 17 Mar. 2023. Web. 29 Jan. 2024.

## About the Author

Justin is a new author who writes fictitious mythological adventure mysteries. His novels are written for a teenage plus audience. His professional engineering knowledge and creativity enhances the books design of boards, the story, and the characters. His books highlight courageous characters whose purpose is to maintain a world order of peace, light and unity for all infinity. His primary characters are teenagers on a quest to discover their true identity, purpose and truth. They do this with their family, friends and faith. His readers are introduced to the boarders of today and of ancient times whose purpose is to battle against evil forces that try to destroy the world's love, goodness, life and light.

The author is a mechanical engineer with experience in designing boards, riding boards and teaching boarders. His learned wisdom is a result of his personal life experiences. His quest to find his true identity and truth was supported by his academic studies, playing sports, outdoor adventures, faith, family and friends.

The author resides in Michigan. He earned a Bachelor of Science in Mechanical Engineering from Michigan Technological University (MTU), in Houghton Michigan, in

2014; and was awarded the MTU Leading Scholar Award from 2010 - 2014.

Follow Justin Dalrymple-Kelly on Facebook @ Dharma Boards Productions. He is the Author of Dharma Boards: Manifesto Part 1 & 2. These two books are the first in the Dharma Board Series. They are available for purchase online; or at no cost as an audio book accessible at https;//m.youtube.com@Dharma Boards Productions. The Dharma Boards: Revolution Part 1 & 2 is now available for purchase online.

Justin can be contacted at jmdalrym@mtu.edu